Alien World
The Xandra
Book 7

Herbert Grosshans

Published by
Melange Books, LLC
White Bear Lake, MN 55110
www.melange-books.com

Cover Design by Fantasia Frog Designs

Prologue

In the thirtieth century Earth was overpopulated and depleted of its natural resources. Thousands of colonists were leaving their home planet in search of a new home. Frozen in cryogenic suspension inside huge colony-ships, they traveled for years waiting to be revived when a suitable planet was found.

The fourth planet circling a G-type star 325 light-years from Earth appeared to be an ideal world to begin a new life for 2,000 men and women. With a diameter of 13,000 km and gravity slightly higher than one G, it was so close to Earth standard as to make it one of the best planets humans had discovered.

Three moons circled the planet, two large ones and one small one.

The colonists named the planet Nu-Eden, believing they had discovered Paradise.

When the humans arrived in the system, they found a huge abandoned space station circling the planet. The station was a thousand years old, apparently built by an unknown alien race.

Of simple design, it was a giant sphere about one-and-a-half km in diameter, studded with twelve towers. Each tower was divided into 25 floors connected through an elevator. At the end of the tower was an observation deck, with transparent walls and ceiling.

The station was not completely inactive when the colonists found it. Even though nothing was working, some kind of power source in the sphere's center was active because there was still gravity.

Each tower was completely sealed off from the main body, accessible only through a pressurized chamber. The engineers on the mother-ship adapted one of those towers to acceptable living conditions. They installed an independent power plant on one of the lower floors. The elevators worked and the tower had lights, heat, and air. Water was brought up from the planet below and stored in huge tanks located on the first floor. From there it was pumped into pipes that ran up to the top of the tower.

Over two hundred men and women now lived aboard the station. They observed the progress of the settlers on Nu-Eden in the two colonies established on the planet, Alpha Colony and Beta Colony, with five hundred settlers living in each colony. Another thousand colonists remained in cryogenic suspension to be awakened after the first wave of settlers were established, which had been estimated to take five years.

There were seventeen planets in the star system ACG 671-397-D. The closest to the Primary was too hot for anything living to exist. The side that faced the Primary had surface temperatures in excess of five hundred degrees Celsius. The second planet wasn't much better—too hot on the sunlit side and too cold on the dark side. The third planet was a giant, with a diameter of 51,000 km. There was some sort of life on it, but no humans could live there.

The first survey of the fifth planet didn't create much excitement with the survey team. It was similar in size to Nu-Eden, a little larger, but not large enough to increase the gravity.

About three-quarters of the planet's surface was land. It had only one ocean, and it was in constant motion. A huge ridge of high mountains ran from north to south, effectively dividing the landmass into two separate continents.

High, rugged mountains covered much of the land surface, but there were also large plains with tall grasses and wild forests. Myriads of long wide rivers snaked through the mountains and flat lands, emptying their vast amounts of water into huge deep inland lakes. It was a rough and savage world, with wide temperature fluctuations between the seasons, plagued in the summer by vicious thunderstorms, hurricanes, and torrential rains, and by severe snowstorms in the winter. A deep blanket of snow or thick ice covered the mountains and the poles.

Shortly after the crew and researchers settled in the space station, Captain Cunningham set up a research station in the Western Hemisphere of the fifth planet where the climate appeared to be more moderate. A team of five men and five women scientists decided to stay on the fifth planet for a year, longer, if they felt the need for it.

A few months later, Cunningham sent a second team consisting of twenty scientists to join the researchers already living there, but Exploration Team Delta under the command of Lt. Striker crash-landed in the mountains on the fifth planet.

On Nu-Eden, the colonists faced a horrible truth. Nu-Eden was already occupied by a sentient entity who called herself Xandra, and she was not willing to share her planet with the humans. Slowly, the Xandra changed the humans by absorbing their bodies and creating identical clones, making them into creatures under her control.

On the space station humans made a remarkable discovery. Deep in the bowel of the station they found fifty humanoid aliens in cryogenic chambers. After the humans brought them out of cryogenic suspension, the aliens identified themselves as the Genaar and told the humans they'd been frozen for a thousand years. The Genaar tried to colonize Nu-Eden, but after the crew on the station found that the colonists on the planet had been changed by a sinister intelligence, they sought refuge in the cryogenic chambers and waited for another ship to rescue them.

However, even with the Genaar's warnings, the humans couldn't prevent the Xandra from invading the space station. The engineers on the mother ship had built a small park with a pond on one of the tower's floor. The water which was brought up from Nu-Eden for the pond contained spores that grew into a large, alien plant—the home of the alien entity. Soon all of the humans on the space station were changed into creatures of the Xandra. Only a handful of soldiers managed to flee and join the Genaar in their cryogenic chambers, hoping some day to be rescued.

Geologist Rob Cameron and his girlfriend Valissa left Alpha Colony to spend time with her parents, but even there they couldn't get away from the influence of the Xandra, so he banded together with a group of other colonists and they planned their escape from Nu-Eden. They captured a space-shuttle after it brought more colonists from the ship and took the journey to the fifth planet where they hoped to find safety and start a new life.

When they stopped at the space station for supplies, they were confronted by a group of Xandra-turned men. In the ensuing short fight Rob's brother Ted was fatally injured and Rob left him behind to be recreated by the Xandra. He knew his brother would lose his humanity, but at least he would still exist.

The fugitives didn't know the research team had discovered the fifth planet also already populated. On one of the research trips, Professor Tennenboum, the leader of the research-station, and his companions came across a group of alien hunters in a fierce battle with one of the savage six-legged, giant cats. The humans saved the life of one of the aliens, who called themselves the Sras. They made friends with the Sras. Irwin Hunter did more than just make friends with them. He spent a passionate night with one of the young Sras females and promised to search and find her again if he ever got the chance.

At the same time, Professor Maisoneuve met with a group of other aliens, the Jnaar. They were descendants of scientists who became stranded on the fifth planet after fleeing from an evil entity on the fourth planet. Thousand years had passed since then. They named their new home Iceworld.

Chapter One

The rush of air entering the space shuttle through the open airlock sent shivers down Rob Cameron's back, not only because the air was laden with ice crystals, but also because it made him realize he was finally free of the Xandra.

He and twenty-one men and women, fled Nu-Eden, the fourth planet in this star system, to escape the influence of the alien entity who called herself Xandra, the Great Mother. They had left Paradise. What would they find on the fifth planet? Would they find the freedom they sought or would this cold planet turn out to be another hell?

Everyone was anxious and excited, and eager to join the men and women already living in the research station.

The screen in the front displayed the outside world with sharp clarity. There wasn't much to look at. Only an oval building like a silvery huge egg dropped onto the thick blanket of snow by some monstrous bird. It lay silent and foreboding, without any signs of life, surrounded by an endless expanse of white, as if waiting for the hatchling inside to break through the shell and climb into the cold, barren world outside.

Cameron shifted his attention to his companions. After spending more than a week in the cramped quarters of a spaceship traveling from Nu-Eden across the dark void of space, he assumed everyone would be eager to leave, but it seemed nobody wanted to be the first one to abandon the cozy warmth and safety of the shuttle.

He couldn't blame them. What waited for them did not look inviting.

"Last time I was here, there wasn't any snow. In fact, this whole area was covered with lush grass and there was no ice on the lake. I have a feeling it's colder here than we expected it to be," Ferd Prowler said, breaking the silence. He was the shuttle pilot who had brought them safely to this planet. The tremendous amount of electrical interference and buffeting winds in the upper atmosphere had made it a rough ride.

Most of the piloting was done by the shuttle's artificial intelligence. The AI took over automatically when it judged it necessary. No human pilot, no matter how capable and skilled, would ever dispute the computer's decision.

Prowler's job was in reality only a backup position.

Cameron chuckled. He would never tell him that. Prowler took his job seriously and didn't like criticism.

"What's that giant egg we see beside the lake?" Conrad, the younger of the Hudson-brothers spoke from behind Cameron.

"That, son, is the research station," Nelson Armand, who sat in the first row, explained, chuckling gleefully. He seemed proud about something. "It looks like an egg, doesn't it? I built that damn thing. That will be our new home for a while. I hope those eggheads inside welcome us with open arms. We're unannounced and unexpected visitors who may upset their cozy little world."

"You built that?" Sigmund Hudson spoke with respect in his voice.

"I sure did." Armand gave another little chuckle. "Not alone, mind you. I was here last year with my crew. Some of them stayed behind when I left. They'll be surprised to see me." His eyes looked thoughtful.

"The place appears deserted," Conrad observed. "Maybe they've left or they're all dead inside."

"I'm sure they're not. They're probably just as eager to stay inside the safety and comfort of the station as we are at the moment in the shuttle." Armand rose to leave his seat. "Let's get dressed for the outside. You all have protective suits. Use them. Judging by the incoming air, it's freezing out there. Nothing like what we're all used to from Nu-Eden."

Cameron turned to look at Valissa. "We made it, Sweetheart."

Her hazel eyes showed her fear, but she smiled bravely. "I didn't think it would be this cold." She hunched her shoulders, shivering.

He laughed. "You're not even outside yet."

People were finally suiting up for the cold. Cameron retrieved his and Valissa's backpack from the overhead compartment and pulled out his suit.

"You heard the man. Better get dressed for the occasion," he joked.

Valissa removed her suit from her pack and stepped into the wide legs. Slipping into the upper part, she tucked her ponytail into the loose-fitting hood and pulled it over her head. Then she sealed the front of the suit by overlapping the magnetic strips.

"I wish this suit wasn't so big," she complained.

"You look attractive in it," Cameron assured her. "Besides, we tried our best to match the suits to everyone on board. We didn't know the exact sizes of everybody nor did we have much time back at the space station when we pilfered all these supplies."

"I know. I worried the whole time you were gone." She smiled mischievously. "By the way, you should know my size better than anyone else." She batted her eyelashes. "After all, your hands have roamed over every part of my body many times."

He laughed and bent to plant a quick kiss on her lips. "I can't wait to do so again," he whispered. "These last two weeks have been murder without holding you in my arms. Mister Lizard is wasting away from being inactive."

She slapped him playfully on the shoulder. "You tell Mister Lizard to be patient. I'm planning to give him plenty of action when the time is right."

Behind them a woman chuckled. Cameron turned to look at Teresa Hudson. The older woman smiled knowingly. "Don't wait too long, girl," she said, her eyes on Valissa. "When a man's lizard is thirsty, he may dip it into another well to quench his thirst, if you know what I mean."

Cameron smiled back at her and gave her a wink with the eye Valissa couldn't see. "You have good ears, Mrs. Hudson. Perhaps I'll have to lower my voice when you're around. My lizard dips into only one well, no matter how many others may be available. I have moral standards, you know." When he looked at Valissa, he saw the rosy color on her cheeks. Putting his arm around her narrow waist, he pulled her close.

Teresa's laugh was friendly. "It's touching to see two young lovers expressing such affection, but remember one thing, young man, this is a small group. We may be the last real humans in this part of the Galaxy. If we want to survive on this planet, we have to look past the moral standards of Earth. Your blushing bride may have to share you with another woman."

"With you?" Valissa said softly.

Teresa shrugged. "With me or perhaps with Natalia or Hillary. How about those two women we picked up at the space station, Zyra and Elini? All of them are young, single, and itching for a man." Her face showed sudden concern. "Don't get me wrong, Valissa. I'm not trying to get between you and Rob. I'm forty-five and I have two wonderful and handsome sons, but I'm not past the childbearing age yet. I just want to give you some well-meant advice. Every woman in our group has to be aware of the fact the only way humans will flourish as a species on this planet is to bear children. You're still young. You have the capacity to bear many children. Should they be all from one father? I don't think that would be wise. We have to mix the gene pool, and it may be a necessity for you or any of the other women to have children with different men. You're very beautiful and your genes should be passed down to as many children as possible. Other men will desire you…have no doubts. You, Rob, you're a handsome man." She smiled. "Even if you hide your face behind a beard. You should have children with different women. The sooner we all face this fact the sooner we will get along much better with each other. There's no room for jealousy in our tribe—our tribe of humans."

"All valid points," Cameron said, feeling uncomfortable with the topic, yet knowing deep inside that Teresa was right. "I believe there's still plenty of time to discuss everything later. Our priority now is to make our presence known to the people already here and hope they make us feel welcome."

"Why would they not be happy to see us?" Valissa looked puzzled.

Cameron shrugged. "They're scientists. Some of them may be happiest if left alone and not bothered by regular folks. These people have been living here for a year now in their cozy little world. They may resent our intrusion."

"You're a scientist. Do you want to be left alone? Is that the reason you go into the wilderness by yourself?"

"I don't mind being alone sometimes." He reached out and touched her cheek. "I'm happiest when I'm with you."

Teresa chuckled. "How romantic. I can see you two are devoted to each other. Let's hope it won't be an obstacle someday. This planet may not allow much romance in our lives."

"We'll take one day at a time," Valissa responded, obviously not enthused about Teresa's remark. "Like Rob said, let's go and meet the people in the research station." She gave Cameron a gentle nudge. "Go. I'm getting hot inside this suit."

They moved down the aisle, following the other passengers. Some had already left the shuttle and were climbing down the narrow ladder. When Cameron reached the exit, he looked down and saw a few people struggling in the deep snow. "We should have brought snowshoes," he said to Valissa, who stood behind him, peering over his shoulder.

"It looks strange to see all this snow, and a little scary." Her voice sounded timid and almost discouraged. "I've never seen snow before. Not in real life I mean."

"I've seen snow," Teresa said, "but never this much. It actually looks quite beautiful. So white and clean. Nothing like the dirty back lanes in Grandchicag where I grew up."

"I think I'm going to like it here." Her son Conrad gazed around. "You could rig up a platform with a sail and zoom across the lake right up to the horizon."

"And get yourself lost in the meantime." His mother's comment dampened his enthusiasm.

Cameron shouldered his backpack and began climbing down. Valissa was close behind him, followed by Teresa and her two sons.

When Cameron jumped off the last step, he sank nearly up to his crotch into the snow. Some of the people already at the bottom laughed, while others cursed loudly, fighting with the white stuff, using their hands to dig themselves out. Cameron looked around to see Gordon Rockwell making a trail away from the shuttle. Rockwell was a big, powerful man, but even he struggled to free his legs.

"I don't think I'll have the strength to make it that far through this deep snow," Claudette Lavallee complained, staring at the distant research station. Her husband Ron Lavallee snorted and tried to follow Rockwell.

"If you were a real man you would offer to carry my pack," his wife said.

He stopped to look back at her. "Sure, I'm good enough to carry your

9

pack," Lavallee sneered, "but not good enough to share your bed. You seem to be doing fine without me. Carry your own pack." He turned away.

"Didn't you bring a sled on board, Rob?" Valissa said to Cameron.

"Yes, we did." Cameron looked up to the open airlock of the shuttle. He saw Rudi Malone behind Zyra Frechette. "Hey, Malone," he called. "How about getting the sled so we can put the packs on it? The snow is so high we're struggling just to move."

Malone disappeared back inside the shuttle. As everyone waited, Teresa and her sons joined the group. She laughed when she couldn't pull her feet out of the snow.

"This looks like more fun than I anticipated," she said, her voice laced with a hint of panic.

Another woman jumped into the snow and tried to move away from the ladder to make room for the people who came behind her. "Wow. I'm not a stranger to snow. We have plenty of it in New-Canada, but this exceeds that by a lot."

Cameron recognized Natalia Laroche, one of the young women Armand had persuaded to come with them to this planet. Her friend Megan Monias came down the ladder a few moments later.

Pausing at the top of the ladder, she studied the snow. "I like to work out but this is not what I expected." Then she laughed and tumbled into the snow beside Natalia.

Malone appeared in the open door to the airlock. "I got the sled," he called. "I'll need someone to help me lower it down."

"I'll give you a hand," Cameron offered. He turned back to the people around him. "Let's clear the area. We don't want any accidents."

A few of the men had trampled down much of the snow by now and it was easier for everyone to move around. It didn't take long to clear an open space in front of the shuttle. Cameron shrugged off his pack and climbed back up the ladder and into the airlock.

"Activate the power unit," he told Malone.

The sled lifted off the floor as soon as Malone switched on the power. "I'll lie on it and work the controls," Cameron offered. "You hang onto the rope and push me outside when I tell you."

Cameron climbed onto the sled and lay down, his head toward the front where the controls were located. Sleds were meant to float close to the surface. This high up there was a chance it could dip to one side if he wasn't careful.

"Go ahead." Cameron had his fingers on the two levers on each side of the small control panel.

Malone pushed the sled carefully out of the lock. It wobbled a little when it slid into the open, but Cameron managed to steady it after a few precarious moments. Slowly decreasing the power, he made the sled sink lower until it floated only about a meter above the snow-covered ground. Sliding off the sled, Cameron let out the breath he'd been holding.

"All right," he called out, "put your packs on the sled. We may not be able to get them all on it, but that's no problem. We'll come back for the rest. Let's get moving, peoples."

They began loading their packs onto the floating platform until it was filled to capacity. Rockwell offered to pull the sled behind him. He was a big, strong man, but his strength was not really necessary, because even loaded up, the sled was easy to pull. It floated on a magnetic field and moved easily in any direction.

Everyone had left the shuttle by now, except for Prowler. After shutting down the engines, he climbed down the ladder to join the people below.

Armand and Malone, also big men, walked ahead of Rockwell to make a trail. Cameron and Valissa walked close behind the sled. Progress was slow, but nobody complained, because everyone knew Armand and Malone had the toughest job of them all. Once the trail was made, walking for the people behind them was fairly easy.

"I think I like walking in a field of high grass much more than this," Valissa said beside Cameron.

He chuckled softly. "At least here you know you're safe. You never know what hides in a field of high grass."

"The grass on Nu-Eden was soft and warm. I could walk barefoot in it. I'm not looking forward to wearing boots all the time."

"You won't have to," a man said behind her. "There isn't always snow on this planet."

Cameron turned his head to look at the pilot. "Prowler, I guess you should know. What was it like then? I heard you say before this valley was covered with lush grass when you were here."

"It was. And the temperature was warm enough to walk barefoot." Prowler laughed quietly. "I personally never had the urge to go barefoot anywhere. I'm quite comfortable wearing boots."

"There are a couple of birds circling above us," a woman called out. "They look big."

Cameron looked into the sky. What he saw sent shivers down his spine. "They're flying high," he said, "but even at this distance it's obvious they're huge. Prowler, what do you know about those birds or whatever they are?"

Prowler shook his head. "Nothing. We never saw anything like that in the sky during all the time we worked here. The only thing one of the men spotted was a large tiger-like animal."

"They're dropping lower," Valissa said.

Everyone stopped moving and watched the two shapes in the sky. Cameron didn't miss the anxiety clearly visible on everyone's face.

"Are they dangerous?" Naomi Lewis stood not far behind Cameron, next to her sister Gabriella.

Their father, Dan Lewis, tried to soothe her fears. "They're birds," he said. "Because of their wide wing span they're probably not as large as they appear from here."

"I don't like them," Gabriella said. "I think I'll go back into the shuttle. Those are huge birds. If they attack us, we'll never make it to the station. Not with all this snow. Besides, we don't even know how to get into that… that egg-thing. It might be locked."

Valissa reached for Cameron's hand. Even through the gloves she wore, he could feel her tremble. "I'm scared, Rob. Gabriella is right. Safety for us lies back in the shuttle. The research station looks deserted. How do we know anyone actually lives in there?"

He squeezed her hand. "If nobody lives in there we'll have the place to ourselves," he joked, but he shared Valissa's fears about the creatures in the sky. They looked like birds, but were they?

"You're right," he said with a low voice to avoid alarming the others. "They are coming closer."

Chapter Two

The snow finally stopped falling until the next snowfall, which would probably come in a matter of days. Wong sat in the upper deck of the research station, staring out of the transparent bubble at the snow-covered landscape surrounding the giant egg he shared with fourteen other people. Nine of them were scientists, one a nurse, and four were construction workers who, like him, had decided to stay behind until the relief shuttle came to pick them up and take them back to the giant space station circling the neighboring planet, the one they had dubbed *Nu-Eden*.

The shuttle never came, and now here he was stuck on a planet covered with ice and snow. Would he ever leave this place again? He had spent many hours trying to contact the space station to no avail. The station stayed silent.

He liked being up here by himself. Not many of the others did. They found it too depressing to see nothing but white outside. It hurt the eyes when you stared for too long at the bleak frozen lake and the snow-capped mountains.

His thoughts drifted to Regina Seagul. He had liked her, finding her flashing dark eyes and olive skin exotic and alluring, but she never showed in interest in him. Then again, he had never indicated he was attracted to her. She was a scientist, interested in alien life-forms, and he was a computer specialist, occupied with his computer and repair drones. They didn't have much in common.

Hard to believe seven months had passed since her disappearance. He hoped she was still alive and busy studying the aliens who abducted her.

He was only half awake when his attention was suddenly aroused by a distant object in the sky. Sitting up, he tried to focus his eyes on it as it raced toward the station, growing in size as it came nearer.

At first, he thought his eyes deceived him or he was hallucinating, but then he nearly shouted with surprise and joy.

The shuttle had finally arrived. It slowed and circled the station once before settling a short distance away from the station.

He shot out of his chair and bounded for the elevator that would take him down to the common room to tell the others.

Perhaps he could go home now. Even if home was only an artificial hollow sphere, but it would take him away from this cold and frozen place.

Professor Tennenboum, the head of the research station, was deeply involved in a discussion with Professor Maisoneuve when Wong burst into the room. The two men were known to get into heated debates sometimes, but this time they were unusually calm and quiet, standing by the small bar each holding a drink. He spotted Irwin Hunter, Jerry Kullmann, and Edmund Zydyk sitting at one of the tables playing cards. At another table sat Vendy Sherbo, Beth McGregor, and Jennifer Ratzenberger. He didn't see any of the others. They were probably busy in the lab or in the library, or possibly in the exercise room.

Hunter looked up as Wong burst into the room. "Hey, Wong, what's going on? You look like you've seen a ghost or something." He waved and grinned.

"No ghost," Wong called out, barely containing his excitement. "The shuttle is here."

Everyone in the room stared at him. "What do you mean by the shuttle is here?" Kullmann demanded.

"The shuttle just landed outside. We can finally leave this miserable rock of ice and snow behind and go back to the space station."

"I suppose we have to send out a welcome-committee," Tennenboum said. "Are the doors open in the tower?"

Wong shook his head. "I don't believe so. I locked them the last time I went outside for the routine maintenance of the cameras. I don't believe anyone else has been outside since then."

"Shouldn't we make sure whoever is in the shuttle is welcome here before we let them enter?" Maisoneuve cautioned.

"It's one of our shuttles," Wong assured him. "Of course, I don't know who's inside. I guess the pilot, probably Prowler, and a couple of workers to help unload the supplies the shuttle is bringing."

"I have to agree with Professor Maisoneuve," Tennenboum said. "Also, I wonder why we never received any news about this shuttle, and why would Captain Cunningham send a shuttle in the winter when the last one they sent never made it?"

"They were lucky to have come at a time when the upper atmosphere in this region of the planet isn't plagued by extreme violent disturbances," Maisoneuve observed.

"Ladies and gentlemen, we have company," a voice said over the speakers. Wong recognized the nasal voice of Yules Bonnet, the meteorologist. He must be sitting at the computer in the control room. It would have alerted him to the presence of the visitor.

"I'm putting it on the screen," Bonnet's voice said again.

The huge screen on one side of the wall sprang to life, displaying the outside world. There was indeed a shuttle sitting on the snow. The exit door was open. People were beginning to emerge and climbing down the ladder. Everyone carried a backpack.

"That doesn't look like a transport shuttle to me," Kullmann remarked. "I don't believe those people are sightseers. It seems we'll be sharing our cozy little home with a bunch of newcomers." He laughed loudly. "I hope there're a few good-looking women among them."

"Good-looking and horny," Zydyk joked. He scowled as he watched the screen. "There seem to be a lot of people."

"I wonder why Captain Cunningham is sending so many people."

Tennenboum voiced what Wong was thinking. It wouldn't surprise him if others thought the same thing. The shuttle that somehow got lost a few months ago, had carried twenty researchers, and from what he could see, there're about that same number of people struggling in the snow. He didn't believe these were the same researchers, though. Somehow, he had a queasy sensation in his stomach, a sense of foreboding. The Captain would not send more researchers to this frozen planet, not in the middle of winter, unless it was some kind of emergency. He knew something was wrong.

He watched as the newcomers tried to make their way toward the station, but it was apparent, they'd be completely exhausted by the time they arrived. Each person carried a large backpack, most likely containing their belongings. The way some of them struggled, it was easy to see the packs were heavy. On the screen, it looked as if the shuttle was close, but he knew that was deceiving. The shuttle was at least half a kilometer away, a long and strenuous trudging through deep, thick snow.

Then somebody lowered a sled out of the shuttle exit door, and the people loaded their packs onto it. They managed to get most of the packs on the floating platform. Then two big men began making a trail, while the others followed slowly behind.

They were too far away to make out individual faces. Everyone wore heavy winter clothing, so it was impossible to tell how many were men and how many were women. Suddenly, they all stopped and looked up into the sky.

Clearly, Bonnet was as curious as anyone watching the screen what the people saw above them. The view shifted and showed a part of the sky.

Kullmann cursed loudly and Wong couldn't blame him. What the screen displayed chilled him and made his fingers curl into fists.

"Krill!" Maisoneuve said into the stunned silence, using the Jnaar word. The humans had dubbed them Roc, after the giant bird in an old Earth legend. It appeared two of them circled above the group of men and women milling in the circle of trampled snow, unaware of the silent death waiting to wreak havoc among them.

"We have to warn them," Beth said. "If those birds attack them they won't stand a chance."

"If they move away too far from the shuttle they will definitely be in grave danger," Tennenboum agreed. He seemed to make a quick decision. "Mister Hunter and Professor Maisoneuve, go take the Roamer and give those people protection. Take out the birds if you have to." His eyes fell on Wong. "Mister Wong, you accompany them. And don't forget the lasers."

Wong nodded. He was as anxious as any of the others to find out who the newcomers were.

The three men donned winter clothing and insulated boots. Maisoneuve and Wong grabbed laser rifles from the armory and made certain they were fully charged. The Landroamer stood in its usual place in the elevator tower. Hunter moved into the driver's seat, while Maisoneuve and Wong sat on the seats behind him.

Using the remote control, Hunter took the elevator down to the ground floor and opened the exit door. Then he eased the Landroamer onto the field of snow outside. Floating on a magnetic cushion, the Landroamer slid easily across the white expanse toward the shuttle.

Wong craned his neck to look into sky. All the windows in the Landroamer were curved at the top, which made it possible to see objects above them. He spotted one of the Roc spiraling lower and worried it might decide to swoop down on the unsuspecting pitifully small humans struggling in the deep snow.

"I have the uneasy feeling that bird is looking for a snack," Hunter said, voicing Wong's thoughts.

"If it goes into a dive, we may be short one visitor," Maisoneuve growled. "Possibly even two."

"We should warn them to go back to the shuttle. They're without any protection in the open like this," Hunter said. He threw a look at Maisoneuve. "Do you think you can hit those birds at this distance, Professor?"

Maisoneuve shrugged. "I can give it a try."

"How about you, Len?" Hunter addressed Wong.

"I'm not that good with a rifle," Wong admitted. "Not at shooting anything so far up, anyway."

"I've shot one of these big birds when I was on a hunt with the Jnaar," Hunter said.

"Well, then be my guest and use my rifle to try your luck again. I'm not sure if these laser rifles are effective at this range, though." Wong watched the circling bird. It dropped even lower.

"When I shot the Roc I was closer than I would ever want to get to a live one again. It presented a large target and wasn't hard to hit. Believe me, they're large." Hunter squinted against the sky. "Is it my imagination or are those birds closer now?"

"You're not imagining it," Wong confirmed Hunter's suspicion.

They had almost reached the group of newcomers.

"Hey, isn't that Prowler?" Wong said.

"I'll be damned, it is," Hunter exclaimed. "There is Mr. Armand. I'm curious what this is all about. This can't be a social visit."

"I suspect these people will be staying permanently," Maisoneuve said. "I wonder, though, why would they choose to come here to this forsaken place instead of going to Nu-Eden?"

The people outside had been watching the Landroamer but not the sky. One of them suddenly pointed up. Others looked also and began pointing. A few turned and began running back to the shuttle, while the closest to the Landroamer struggled through the snow in search of protection from the menace above their heads.

"Something is happening out there," Wong shouted. He ripped open the door and jumped outside, his laser rifle ready. He was only barely aware of Maisoneuve doing the same thing. He sank into the snow and fought for a moment to keep his balance. Acting instinctively, he brought up his laser rifle and aimed it at the huge shadow swooping down from above.

The Roc came toward them with frightening speed, growing in size. Tracking the huge body, he squeezed the firing stud. A bolt of white-hot lightening left the weapon but missed the target.

Only a couple of seconds later Maisoneuve fired his laser. The beam from his weapon sliced through one of the wings. The huge bird lost its balance. It veered off to one side and tried to lift back into the air, but the loss of half its wing made it impossible for it to rise. It sailed away and crash-landed some distance from the shuttle. Wong saw it struggling in the snow, flapping its wings but to no avail. It was stranded on the ground, clearly never to fly again, but it wasn't dead.

"It's down," Hunter observed. He had joined them outside and stood buried to his hips in the snow. "We should go and kill it. That's a lot of meat. Would be a shame to let it go to waste."

Wong checked the sky and didn't see the second Roc anymore. It must have decided to seek for food elsewhere.

The first of the new people had reached them. One of the two big men making a trail for the sled pulled by another big man was Nelson Armand. He grinned at Wong.

"You need more practice, Wong. That was a large target and hard to miss."

Wong grinned back. "Hey, Boss, we've expected you to pick us up a little earlier. You're about nine months late."

"I never intended to come back. Did the second shuttle not arrive?"

18

Armand peered at Wong, questions in his eyes.

Wong shook his head. "It never did. Apparently, it crash-landed somewhere on this planet. We never heard from any of them."

"Too bad. There were some good people on that shuttle," Armand said wistfully. "We can't afford to lose anyone. Too much is at stake."

Wong lifted his chin to indicate the group of people behind Armand. "Who are your friends?"

"Fugitives from Nu-Eden just like me."

"I don't understand. What do you mean by fugitives?"

"We'll explain everything later." Armand turned to look over the small crowd milling around behind him. "Right now, we're all anxious to get into the station. One week with so many people in the cramped quarters of the shuttle is a long time. I hope you have room for us."

"There's plenty of room. You shouldn't even have to ask that question, Boss. I mean you probably know every inch of this place."

Armand nodded. "I do. It was just a routine question. Are we welcome is what I really meant."

"Of course you're welcome." He grinned. "Even if you weren't, we have no choice but to open our arms. I hope you brought a few good-looking women, at least."

"They're all good-looking." Armand chuckled and let his gaze wander to Hunter, who had been listening to his conversation with Wong but had stayed silent. "Glad to see you too, Hunter."

Hunter raised a hand. "Welcome to Iceworld, Boss. I have this terrible feeling my stay here will be a bit longer than anticipated."

Armand smiled grimly. "I'm afraid so. It looks like we'll be here permanently, or at least until the next ship from Earth arrives."

"Four years from now. A long time." Hunter's smile looked equally grim. "I don't know if I'll survive that."

"Gentlemen, I think it's time to stop this chit-chat," Maisoneuve growled. "We should get these people out of the cold and into the safety of the station. The second Roc may come back, perhaps with friends. We don't know much about those birds and their habits."

"All right, let's go." Armand lifted an arm to signal the silently watching group.

Wong joined Hunter and Maisoneuve in the shuttle. Hunter turned the vehicle around and headed back to the station, keeping at low speed. Looking back, Wong saw the small group of men and women following and fighting the deep snow.

It took nearly twenty minutes until everyone arrived at the tower that led into the station. Maisoneuve jumped out of the Landroamer to direct traffic. Not everyone fit into the elevator, but they squeezed into it until there wasn't any room to turn. The few who were left behind, watched the doors close with eager and longing eyes.

Wong and Hunter stayed inside the Landroamer, keeping a watchful eye on the sky, just in case the Roc made another appearance. When the elevator came back down the rest of the newcomers piled into it. The only ones left outside were Armand and the big man with the sled heaped with backpacks.

Armand approached the Landroamer and Wong opened the door. "There are still a number of packs left beside the shuttle. Do you think you can pick them up with the Roamer? It would make it much easier."

"No problem," Hunter said from his place behind the controls. Easing the Landroamer cautiously away from the tower, he headed for the shuttle.

Getting closer to the shuttle, Wong spied a tall, lonely figure standing beside the small mountain of backpacks. Hunter stopped the Landroamer beside the packs and he and Wong got out.

The lone guardian of the packs lifted a hand in greeting. "I was wondering if anyone would come back for me," he said with a tiny grin.

Wong smiled at the tall man. "Prowler, we should have known you're the one who brought the shuttle down safely through that hellish weather up there in the atmosphere. One would think once is enough. I'm surprised you came back to this place."

"I would have preferred not to return, but circumstances beyond my control forced it on me." The pilot shook himself. "All this snow makes me cold. I grew up in Panama and I'm not used to snow. I'm also not used to this fogging cold. It would be nice to curl up in front of a warm fireplace."

Hunter laughed. "Keep on dreaming, Prowler. No fireplace in there. Only sterile walls made from plastasteel, but the temperature is pleasant and warm. It'll be a bit more crowded with all the newcomers, but we'll manage. I'm looking forward to the company of different people. I was getting lonely and a bit bored."

They loaded the packs into the Landroamer and then took off back to the station.

"It looks bleak out there," Prowler remarked, staring out of the window. "Bleak and cold. I was hoping for better weather."

"I have more good news," Hunter said. "Prepare yourself for at least another nine months of this." The trip was short and he parked the Landroamer in front of the closed elevator doors. Using the remote control, he brought down the elevator. Then he drove into the tower.

When they climbed out of the Landroamer, Prowler threw back his hood and looked around. "I didn't think I'd ever see the inside of this place again. I was hoping to retire on Nu-Eden."

"Why didn't you?" Wong asked.

"Nu-Eden turned out to be Hell. So has the space station. We may be the only True-Humans left. I wasn't going to hang around until the Xandra turned me into one of her creatures."

"The Xandra? Who or what is the Xandra?"

"It seems Nu-Eden was not the ideal planet we assumed. It was already occupied. We have a lot to tell you, but wait until we're settled."

Wong remembered Armand's ominous words about being fugitives. It appeared things had gone terribly wrong on the space station and on the fourth planet. He wanted to hear more about it.

Most of the newcomers had already left the tower. Only the ones whose backpacks had been left behind waited for them. Wong and Hunter unloaded the packs and then parked the Landroamer in its usual spot.

"I'm going to talk to Professor Tennenboum and ask him what he wants to do about the bird we shot," Hunter told Wong. "He may want you to come along to finish it off and slaughter it."

"Perhaps he wants to come along himself," Wong suggested. Then he grinned. "He might want to be away from the Station for a little while and let somebody else handle the integration of the new people into our cozy little world."

Chapter Three

Cameron examined his and Valissa's new quarters. The room was spacious enough for both of them, but the thought he might spend the rest of his life in these cramped, sterile quarters dampened his good spirits a little. They had one wide bed, which could be turned into a couch or stowed inside the wall to create more space in the room, a desk, a couple of chairs, and a closet just large enough to store their meager possession of clothing and a few other items. A screen in one of the walls allowed them to view plays and get information from the station's mother computer. It could even display the area around their new home should they feel the desire to check out conditions on the outside. It was like having a window; an illusionary window, because there weren't any real ones in the rooms. All outside walls were smooth and solid to protect the inhabitants from the perils and dangers of a hostile environment. The research station was built like a spaceship, totally isolated from the outside world.

Used to spending his time in open spaces with the wide sky above him, he hoped he wouldn't find this place turning into a prison. He needed to see the sun and clouds during the day and the stars at night. Maybe he should have stayed on Nu-Eden after all. The Xandra had promised she would not change anyone who did not wish so.

The Xandra. Would she keep her promise?

Valissa lay stretched out on the bed, apparently asleep. He leaned back in the chair and closed his eyes, remembering the disturbing vision the Xandra had shown him…

After taking a bath in the pond, he walked back toward shore and climbed onto dry land. Looking down at his nude body, he felt he should get dressed, even though there wasn't anyone around to see him. As he headed for the huts, he heard splashing behind him and turned to see what caused it. While he looked across the pond, a snorting sound made him whirl around. Something heavy smashed into his legs and he stumbled forward. Pain tore through his body as sharp tusks ripped open his thigh. He tried to fight off his attacker but lost his balance and fell to the ground. He screamed as the creature slashed its razor-sharp tusks across his belly. Darkness descended swiftly, took away the terrible pain...

His awareness shifted. He seemed to float in the air, looking down at a naked man lying lifeless on the soft ground. Blood spurted from his shredded thigh, painting the leaves and grass around him red. Entrails spilled out of a huge gap in his torn belly. A large, pig-like animal with curved tusks stood over the man, ripping pieces of flesh from the bloody thigh.

The beast lifted its bloodstained snout and let out a piercing scream as a number of small creatures dropped out of the trees. He recognized them. The humans called them Tree-elves. They carried long sticks with sharpened ends which they used to stab at the animal. It ran at them, snorting and bellowing, but they were quick, darting out of the way. Their pointy sticks left puncture wounds in the beast's hide and it finally ran off into the jungle.

The Tree-elves lifted the bloody mass that had once been a man and carried him into the water of the pond, toward the plant where the Great Mother lived.

The man had Rob's face...

He would have died that day in the jungle, but the Xandra repaired his wounds, replaced parts of his body, and gave him a new leg. However, it came with a cost. She used him as a spy. Because of him she knew about their plans to escape Nu-Eden, yet, she did not stop them, and even wished him good luck.

Had she been sincere? What were her motives? The humans considered her an evil entity, but was she?

He didn't know. The contact with her broke when he fled her planet. He was finally free of her.

When he heard Valissa stirring on the bed, he opened his eyes.

"I must have fallen asleep," she said, sitting up. Rubbing her eyes, she turned lazily. "We're finally alone," she said with a sly smile. "You know what I feel like doing right now?"

He knew what she was going to say but feigned comprehension. "Sleep?"

She laughed and rolled to the edge of the bed. Her hazel eyes gave him a mock stare.

"Don't act as if you don't know, Mister Rob Cameron. It's been over two weeks since you and I were intimate. I'm horny and I need a virile man right now."

He grinned. "Then this is your lucky day, young lady. I can give you half an hour."

She pouted. "Only half an hour? Is that all?"

"I'm afraid so. We'll have to be at the orientation meeting in about an hour." Smiling, he rose and stood beside the bed, looking down at her. "I may not even last that long. I think I'm ready to explode with all the built-up pressure."

Chuckling, she lifted her arms. "Then come into my arms. As long as you'll explode inside me I'll be happy." She shifted her position on the bed to make room for him.

He lay down beside her and took her into his arms, kissing her gently.

She kissed him back with pent-up passion before breaking the kiss. "I need to feel your naked skin on mine. Let's not waste precious time like this."

Her hands went to his belt and began unbuckling it. Pushing down his pants, she touched his half-erect penis. Giggling, she stroked it into the hardness of an iron rod.

"I think he's looking for a soft place," she whispered breathlessly, her fingers clamping tightly around his stiff organ.

Letting go of him, she slipped out of her shirt, baring her breasts. Then she pulled off her pants. Naked, she lay back and looked up at him, an expectant smile on her full lips.

"Let me take off my shirt, too," he said, his voice hoarse. Looking at her lovely, exposed body, he groaned. "I've forgotten how beautiful you are. I wish we had more time. I could look at you for hours and never tire of it."

"We have our whole life in front of us." Her eyes were solemn. "I hope you'll always look at me this way."

"I will, I promise." He put his hand over her breast and squeezed it gently. Gliding his hand across her flat stomach, he cupped her clean-shaven Venus-mound. "You have a lovely pussy," he whispered, putting a finger between her pussy-lips and rubbing gently.

She moaned and lifted her hips. "That feels nice, but I want more."

"Be patient," he whispered, controlling his urge to plunge his stiff organ into her without any foreplay. "I'll have to heat you up first."

Laughing softly, she squeezed his finger with her labia. "I'm so hot down there you could boil an egg."

He bent over her and took one of her nipples between his teeth, teasing it gently. Then he began kissing the valley between her breasts. Sliding his tongue across her soft skin, he let it travel across her belly down to her puffy mound. He licked her stiff clitoris, making her moan and thrash around on the bed.

"Put it in me now," she cried out. "Don't wait any longer."

He didn't need any encouragement. Moving between her spreading thighs, he pressed his hard manhood between her swollen pussy-lips. She was more than ready for him. Pushing forward, he slid easily into her. A satisfied little cry escaped her lips as she accepted him. He grunted and began moving on top of her.

It didn't take long before she whipped her lower body against him, moaning loudly. Dousing him with her warm liquid, he knew she was experiencing an orgasm. He cupped her taut buttocks and hammered into her with powerful strokes.

"Ohh... ohh... this feels so good," she whimpered, her wails sounding like that of a distressed fawn.

She lifted her hips to take him deeper into her and crushed her arms around his back, raking his skin feverishly with clawed hands. His fingers dug into her rotating buttocks and, with a loud shout, he gave in to the demands of his own tortured body, flooding her womb with his hot discharge. The pleasure was intense and wonderful, and he loved the woman in his arms with his whole being for giving him such joy.

Collapsing into her embrace, he lay on top of her slick body, breathing harshly.

"That was beautiful and satisfying," she said softly. "I love you so much."

"I love you, too," he told her. "I hope nothing ever comes between us to take this love away."

She kissed him. "Nothing ever will," she whispered. "Our love will endure forever."

He rolled onto his back. Staring at the ceiling, he wondered about that, hoping she was right. He recalled what Teresa Hudson told Valissa after they landed. "We have to mix the gene pool and it may be a necessity for you or any of the other women to have children with different men. There's no room for jealousy in our tribe—our tribe of humans."

Would he be able to accept that? He wasn't sure. Love is a strong emotion. So is jealousy. The history of humankind was full of atrocious acts committed by jealous lovers.

He knew he loved Valissa deeply. Remembering the first night by the pond on Nu-Eden, he recalled how he had been enthralled with her immediately. On the second night, they proclaimed their love for each other. Their emotions had been fueled by the scent of the purple flowers and the sight of the red moon. He accepted that, but he also knew his feelings for her had been real. Now, here, on this alien planet, millions of kilometers away from the Xandra's control, there was nothing to influence their thoughts. His thoughts were his own. His love for Valissa was as strong as ever, perhaps even more so.

Would she love him still if she knew he betrayed their love with Jirina? How would she react if she found out he got Jirina pregnant that night when they visited Jirina's parents? How about the night he had sex with her girlfriend Coletta? Or the final act of betrayal when he fogged her sister-in-law Leezi? Even though they had been under the spell of the Xandra, he felt guilty. He wished it had never happened.

"What are you thinking?" Valissa asked.

He turned his head to look into her eyes. Smiling, he reached out to touch her cheek. "Nothing important, my love, and nothing to worry about." He sat up and looked at his timepiece. "We'd better hurry. I wish we had time to take a shower." He chuckled. "You've made be work up a sweat."

She slapped his chest. "Are you calling making love to me work? It should be pure pleasure and nothing else."

"It was pure pleasure. It always is." He looked down at her with a mock-leer. "If you don't cover up that delectable body of yours I shall ravish you again, young lady."

She laughed. "With that limp thing of yours? I hope he'll be usable again tonight. I have plans."

He slipped from the bed and reached for his clothes. "So have I," he said, grinning.

* * * *

Professor Tennenboum hadn't shown any interest in accompanying Hunter and Wong to collect the downed Roc. He needed to greet the newcomers to get them acquainted with routines and have them settled into their new home, a task he wasn't going to leave for someone else. This left Hunter and Wong alone with the chore of ensuring the giant bird was dead and to bring the carcass to the Station. With all these added mouths to feed, the unexpected large quantity of fresh meat was a welcome and pleasant addition to the food supply. It would last for a few months in the freezer.

They took out the Landroamer again, and this time they hooked the flatbed to the back of the vehicle. It would make it easier to load the chunks of meat onto an open platform instead of trying to pack it into the Landroamer's storage compartment.

They didn't run into any difficulties spotting their quarry. The dark shape of the Roc was visible even without the use of binoculars. They stopped the Landroamer a short distance away and jumped outside. Strapping on snowshoes, they slowly walked toward the wary giant bird.

The Roc was down but not dead. Lying on top of the snow with its good wing spread wide and the stump of the severed one partially hidden, it clacked its beak in warning when the two men approached. The fall from the sky had most likely stunned it, but even with the severed wing it was not injured enough to be harmless. It could still inflict serious and deadly wounds with the long, sharp claws on its massive feet or its huge beak.

"It looks much bigger from this close," Wong observed.

"Let's not get any closer," Hunter warned. "That beak is sharp enough to take your head off with one swipe."

Wong lifted his laser rifle. "I have no intention of giving it the chance. Let's put it out of its misery."

Hunter nodded and brought up his own rifle. Aiming at the head of the bird he squeezed the trigger of his weapon and unleashed a bundle of pure energy that burned off half the feather-covered skull. Wong's shot took care of the other half. Part of the beak dropped into the snow. The cauterized stub of the long neck hung for a moment in the air before it also sank into the snow. A shudder went through the rest of the body, the good wing fluttered viciously, throwing large amounts of snow into the air, and then the great body of the Roc lay still.

Wong approached the dead bird cautiously and stood looking down at it. "Have you ever gutted something this big?"

Hunter let out a chuckle. "I've gutted larger prey than this, my friend, but never a bird this huge."

"You grew up on Emerald, right? I heard it's a savage world."

"Savage and wild." Hunter's laugh was tainted with pangs of sadness as memories rose up inside him.

"Like this one?"

"My home world is nothing like this planet. Our year is much shorter and the seasons are more moderate. Mind you, we have violent storms and hurricanes at times and the land is rugged over most of Emerald." He sighed. "I miss it. I wonder if I'll ever set foot on it again."

"Well, the next ship from Earth is supposed to be here in four years. Not such a long time." Wong threw his friend a long look. "At least you have your invisible companion to remind you of your ex-girlfriend. It's almost like having her here with you."

Hunter's gaze wandered to his wrist and to the gadget strapped to it. "Dawn isn't invisible. I can make her appear any time I want her."

Wong shook his head. "She's not real, Irwin. Just a hologram."

"Much more than a mere hologram. Much more," Hunter assured him.

"If you say so. You never showed her to me, but if it makes you happy to stare at a three-dimensional projection who am I to judge. Myself, I prefer a live woman," Wong said wistfully, looking toward the forest in the north, a far look in his eyes. "A woman I can touch and hold in my arms."

Hunter knew what Wong was thinking. "Too bad about Regina," he said, softly. "I knew you had a thing for her."

Wong shook himself out of his momentary trance. "I did, but she's gone now. She'll never know how I felt." He bent down to touch the thick mantle of feathers covering the Roc's body. "Let's get started. I don't want to be out here when it gets dark."

Hunter agreed and joined Wong. Pulling his hunting knife from its sheath, he looked at it, wondering if it would be sharp enough to penetrate the thick skin of the big bird, but then he remembered the day when he accompanied the Jnaar youths to hunt Thrall, the small, deer-like herbivores, and the Roc he shot out of the sky. They had gutted and cut it apart with their primitive knives. He shouldn't have any problems cutting this one with a knife made from superior, nearly indestructible steel. The only obstacle would be the sheer size of the carcass. It would be difficult to manhandle it. They should have asked for a couple of men to come along.

"We'll have to slice off the wings first so we can turn it onto its back," he said.

Wong used his laser to cut through the joints where the wings were attached to the body. Then they dragged the severed wings away and began the task of moving the carcass into position to give Hunter access to the belly area.

"Those are quite some drumsticks," Wong joked. "I wonder if the meat is as dark as that of a turkey."

"A turkey?"

"Yeah, a turkey. We eat them for Thanksgiving where I come from. You've never eaten turkey?"

Hunter straightened up from his bent position and took a breather. Even though the knife went in easy it was still a grueling task to cut the heavy layer of fat covering the tough skin underneath.

"No, I haven't. I assume it's a bird. We don't have them on Emerald."

"Too bad. They taste great..." Wong stopped talking abruptly. "We've got company."

Hunter turned to look in the direction Wong pointed. At first he thought it was a vehicle heading toward them, but then he saw two figures wrapped in furs walking in front of some kind of contraption. They walked bent over and it became evident they were pulling a sled across the snow.

The travelers were obviously aware they had been spotted. They stopped for a moment to look at the two men watching them, but then they carried on, pulling their heavy load behind them. Their movements were slow, but they seemed determined to get to wherever they were heading.

As they came closer, Hunter saw that one was definitely a male and the other, the smaller one, a female or a young boy. They wore fur hats. A piece of thin, soft leather hid half the face of the smaller one, but judging from their large eyes it was clearly apparent they were not human. They were members of the alien race known as Jnaar.

Hunter had been wondering how they managed to move across the snow without sinking. He recognized their footwear, pieces of leather strung over branches bent into oval shapes strapped to the bottom of their boots, as the equivalent of his and Wong's snowshoes.

The newcomers stopped about ten meters from them. The man had a bow slung across his back, but he made no moves to indicate he might use it. He spread his arms wide.

"Arula," he said.

His large purple eyes studied the two men. He showed no fear, even though his facial expression indicated his surprise at finding two strangers to his world. Two aliens who shouldn't be here.

Hunter understood the word. It meant peace. He imitated the man's gesture. "Arula."

The man slapped his right fist into his left shoulder. "Raaskar." Then he indicated his companion. "My daughter Raas-ini."

Realizing, he still held the knife in his hand, Hunter folded and sheathed it. He touched his left shoulder. "Hunter and this is Wong," he said in Jnaar.

Raaskar gave him an astonished stare. "You speak our language?"

"Yes, I spent some time with your people before the snow fell and I learned your language."

"You must have been with them a long time."

"Not long but enough to learn the basics."

Hunter didn't tell him about Dawn, the computer strapped to his wrist, which had been essential to help him learn and absorb the Jnaar language so quickly. How could he explain such technology to a primitive man?

"Where are you coming from and what is your destination? Are there more of your people traveling across the snow?"

"No. We're alone now. We were hunting in the mountains. There were many of us, but when the time came to return to our winter-home, our tribe left without us."

"So you were part of a larger group?" Hunter wondered why a tribe would leave some of their members behind. "Why did you not go with the rest of your people? Are you an outcast?"

Raaskar shook his head, his lips turning into a tight smile. "No outcast. My mate was injured and could not be moved. My daughter and I stayed with her until she was almost healed before we dared to make the long journey."

"Where is your mate now?"

Raaskar turned and pointed at the tent made from animal skins on top of the sled. "In there. She is unable to walk on the snow for long distances. Her foot did not heal properly." He gave Hunter a calculating look. "You killed a Krill. There is much meat on the body. I would be grateful for some of the meat. In exchange, I will help you with butchering it."

"Your help would be welcome and we would be happy to share some of the meat with you, but perhaps you want to come with us into our winter home. You could rest for a while. We have a woman skilled in medicines who could examine your mate and possibly help her with the healing," Hunter suggested.

The Jnaar looked at the giant egg of the Station. "Is that where you live?"

"Yes."

"There are many of you?"

"Yes, there are, but not so many that there isn't enough room for you to stay with us."

Wong coughed beside Hunter. "Shouldn't you run this by Professor Tennenboum first?" he said in a low voice.

"I don't believe he'll object but go ahead, contact him and tell him about our visitors."

"Why don't you? You've got that thing strapped to your wrist."

"Okay." Hunter lifted his wrist to his lips. "Dawn, you heard Wong," he said into the gadget. "Get Professor Tennenboum on the com."

He heard Dawn's soft chuckling inside his head. "I'm way ahead of you, Hunter. He's been listening in to your conversation since I called him."

"Mr. Hunter, I understand you've invited some guests." Tennenboum's voice came from the speaker loud enough for everyone to hear.

"Yes, I have. I didn't think you'd deny help to people in need, Professor," Hunter said with a low voice, throwing a glance at Wong. "This is what I wanted to avoid," he said and looked at Raaskar, but the Jnaar didn't show any signs of distress. "What do you suggest we do, Professor?"

"The only thing you can. Bring those people here."

Letting out a slow sigh, Hunter relaxed. "Will do. See you later. It may be a while."

"That was our leader," he explained to Raaskar. "He offers you our hospitality. It would be wise for you to accept. We can help your mate. I'm sure all three of you are tired from your journey."

He rubbed his cold hands together in an effort to get the blood circulating. The wind was blowing from the north and the temperature seemed to be dropping.

"Let's get on with the job of butchering this bird."

"May I check on my mate first?" Raaskar asked. "She should be awake by now."

"Of course you may. I would like to meet her."

Raaskar pulled away the piece of leather that closed the entrance to the tent. Somebody moved inside the darkness of the interior and then a fur-covered head appeared in the entrance, followed by a body clad in thick furs. Large, purple eyes looked at Hunter out of a woman's thin face and a pair of full but pale lips gave him a friendly smile.

The woman turned to her husband. "I listened to your conversation," she said with a soft, but somewhat strained voice. "Let us go with these strangers. I am weary and in pain. These walls you've made for me protect me from the blowing winds, but they do not keep out the cold. My body is as cold as the frigid waters of a mountain stream. I cannot go on much longer."

Like all the Jnaar females Hunter had met, this one was no exception. She had a haunting beauty about her and it was difficult to judge her age.

She turned the gaze of her bright eyes to Hunter. "We will accept your invitation. Thank you, stranger."

"My name is Hunter," he told her.

She inclined her head. "And I am Laneea."

"Laneea," he repeated. "A beautiful name befitting a beautiful woman." He smiled and looked at Raaskar. "Perhaps your mate would like to sit in our vehicle to warm up while we cut up the Krill?"

The Jnaar seemed to hesitate, but then he shrugged. "It is her choice." His eyes were wistful when he looked at Laneea. "If it is your wish we will follow these men into their home. I feel regret I could not protect you from the cold."

Her smile did not show resentment. "You brought me here and I live. That is all I can ask. Now I would like to sit in their odd-looking sled so I can warm my frozen body." She crawled into the open and stepped off the sled to sink into the deep snow.

Raaskar went to her, scooped her up in his arms, and held her close. "I will carry you." His snowshoes sank deeper into the snow as he carried the additional weight, but he managed to get her to the Landroamer without stumbling and falling.

Hunter walked closely behind them and opened the door to the vehicle. Raaskar put his mate into one of the rear seats. His daughter followed them.

"Would it be all right if I joined my mother?" she asked in a small voice. "I also feel tired and cold."

Raaskar looked at Hunter, who nodded in agreement. "Go ahead."

The girl slid into the seat beside her mother, throwing a quick grateful glance at Hunter. Before he closed the door, he got a glimpse of the girl's face when she pulled off the piece of leather she wore for protection against the cold winds. The brief glimpse was enough to make him realize her delicate beauty. She looked younger than he'd expected and he wondered how she had managed to keep up with her father pulling the heavy sled across kilometers of snow.

Both men walked back to carry on with the job at hand. Hunter was soon grateful for the extra muscle. Sharing some of the meat with the Jnaar family would be a small price to pay in exchange for making a grueling job a lot easier.

Chapter Four

The days on Iceworld, as the natives called the fifth planet in this star system, were exactly 4.8 hours longer than an Earth day. Even after having spent months now with the longer days, Tennenboum's system still had not fully adjusted to the cycle, and some of the others also complained about feeling disoriented and tired at times.

Looking at the screen built into one wall in his relatively tiny quarters, he watched the displayed picture of the outside world for a while and noted it was snowing again. This was their first winter. Only two months had passed since the first snow began falling. They could look forward to eight more months of winter, which meant the worst of the winter was probably still ahead. He was not a stranger to harsh weather, after spending seven years on Alpha Centauri IV, a planet more rugged than Iceworld, but with seasons much shorter and the winters not as cold. Fall had been the most violent season there, with fierce storms and tornados so destructive spaceships were not able to land without facing obliteration. The only time to bring shuttles and small spaceships down safely was during the summer months.

Remembering his time there did not make it more pleasant on Iceworld. He was not anxious to be cooped up inside the Station for another eight months, possibly even longer. Perhaps the arrival of the twenty people was a blessing. It would create more diversion in their daily lives and make it a bit more interesting.

Then, of course, there was the matter of the three Jnaar. He had not met them yet. As far as he knew, there was one male and two females; one suffering from an injury that needed treatment. Hunter and Wong had been late coming back to the station with the butchered Roc and he too busy interviewing the people from the shuttle.

He made it a point of talking to each one separately just to find out with whom he was dealing. All of them seemed to be upright citizens, and there should be no problems integrating them into the routine of the Station. He was pleased to discover a real doctor among them. It would make life much easier for Vendy Sherbo, who was only a nurse. The computerized medical doctor, the CMD, could handle most cases and emergencies, but a computer could never replace the human factor when dealing with patients.

He had also been pleased to see Nelson Armand among the arrivals. Armand knew the Station like the back of his hand, since he had supervised its construction, not to mention that Tennenboum had forged a real friendship with the big man during his stay on Iceworld.

He looked at himself in the small mirror and smiled. Perhaps things would not be as gloomy from now on. The disappearance of Regina Seagul had thrown a dark shadow over the Station and many of the researchers were questioning their purpose on this planet.

After interviewing the new people, he wondered about that himself. According to them, the space station was dead as far as they were concerned, and the fourth planet, Nu-Eden, posed a mortal threat to the humans. If he understood them correctly, there were hardly any True-Humans left on Nu-Eden. They told him about a mysterious woman who called herself Xandra. Apparently, she changed the humans on Nu-Eden and on the space station into some kind of Pseudo-Humans.

He did not know what to make of it. It almost sounded like a conspiracy or some crazy fantasy. Most of the reports were sketchy and without much evidence. Only two of them claimed to have met this alien woman personally, a guy named Rockwell and a geologist, Rob Cameron. He remembered him because he sported a beard, something not common with most men. He needed to speak to these two men privately to get more details on this situation.

Closing the door to his quarters behind him, he walked down the corridor looking forward to his breakfast. When he stepped into the mess hall, he was somewhat taken aback seeing all the people at the tables, even though he had expected it. After all these months with only fourteen other people for company it would take some time to get used to such a large crowd.

He spotted Hunter and Wong with the three Jnaar at one of the tables and headed for them. This would be a good time to get to know them. He noted they wore shirts and pants, obviously not their own. Had it not been for their large, purple eyes, they would not have been distinguishable from the humans.

Hunter gave him a friendly smile. "Good morning, Professor Tennenboum. Will you be joining us at our table?"

"If you don't mind." He took the chair across from Wong and looked at the Jnaar male, who returned his look with the same curiosity on his handsome face. He realized the alien man would not understand him, but he offered a greeting anyway. "Welcome to our home. I hope you're enjoying our hospitality."

The Jnaar turned to look at Hunter and spoke a few words. Hunter answered him in the same language, obviously translating what Tennenboum had said. Turning back to Tennenboum, the man showed his teeth in a smile. "Raaskar," he said, pointing at his chest with his left hand. Then followed a string of words, which, of course, Tennenboum didn't understand.

"He says his name is Raaskar," Hunter translated. "He also wants you to know he gratefully accepts our offer to let him stay here until his mate has been helped."

Tennenboum nodded, turning his attention briefly to the woman beside Raaskar. He was not surprised by her extreme beauty. It seemed all of the Jnaar females were beautiful, judging by the ones he had seen with the group of Jnaar that had come to the place with the ruins, their holy place, before moving into their winter home in the mountain caves. The younger woman, their daughter, was no less lovely.

He tore his gaze away from the Jnaar female, not wanting to stare at her longer than was necessary. "Tell him, our doctor will try her best to heal his mate's injury."

He'd have to speak to the new doctor and make certain she could actually help this woman. If not, perhaps with the help of the CMD they'd be able to do something.

Hunter relayed the message to the alien man. "I took the liberty of supplying our guests with clothing from the stores. I hope you don't mind." He smiled mischievously. "I couldn't let them walk around in here wearing their own clothing. The problem was they were nearly naked underneath their furs. They don't wear underwear the way we do."

Tennenboum smiled back, throwing a quick glance at the two females.

It wouldn't have bothered him to see them naked. He quickly dismissed the thought. "I'm glad you took care of that, Mr. Hunter. How did it turn out with the giant bird you shot?"

The black man shrugged. "We left the meat in the cooler, but somebody will have to cut it into manageable pieces, package it, and put it into the freezers before it spoils."

"How about you look after that," Tennenboum suggested. "You have experience with butchering wild animals."

"I do, but I could use some help. It's a grueling job."

Beside him, Wong lifted both hands. "Don't look at me. I'm not really an experienced outdoorsman. Helping you yesterday out there in the cold and seeing all that blood will last me for a while. Anyway, I know nothing about cuts of meat."

"Perhaps Mr. Armand can help me," Hunter said. "He's hunted big animals on other planets. He'll know what to do."

Tennenboum nodded his approval, remembering the big foreman of the construction crew telling him about his adventures and hunts. "Go ahead and do that. Ask Miss Swornson to give you a hand. She's been doing a fantastic job cooking up some descent meals."

"That she has," Hunter agreed. "I had no idea she was such a fantastic cook. She gave me the impression she was only interested in her bugs and toning her body." His grin did not hide what else he thought about her.

"Sometimes people surprise us." Tennenboum's eyes flicked in the direction of the table where Antje Swornson sat with Beth McGregor and Vendy Sherbo. She seemed deeply involved in a discussion with the other two women. One could be fooled by her athletic body and believe she was more interested in physical activity than the study of animals or, more precisely, bugs. She was an entomologist and a powerhouse of knowledge when it came to insects and other creepy-crawlies. Unfortunately, with the long winter, her studies of the local insect population had come to a halt, so she occupied her time playing the cook and experimented with collected herbs and spices. She seemed to have a talent for it.

As if becoming aware of his scrutiny, the tall woman looked in his direction. Her eyes met his and she gave him a quick smile. She was like that, and even though she had a soft, friendly face, her bright blue eyes gave the impression of being frigid and unapproachable, but Tennenboum knew better. She hid her passionate nature behind that cool exterior, as if trying to fend off anyone who might come too close.

He was fifty-six years old and twenty-two years her senior, but it seemed she was more interested in older men than men her own age. He found that out one night. She wanted to discuss with him in private something about her discoveries, and so he invited her to come to his suite. After consuming a few glasses of wine, they started talking about their personal lives, one thing led to another, and they ended up in his bed together. She spent the night, dispelling the myth about her being frigid and cold.

That was the only time. They didn't talk about the incident after that, but she never gave him any indication she might be interested in spending more intimate hours with him, and neither did he give any to her. Maybe she waited for him to make the next move.

He looked at the plates of the aliens at his table. "I hope they like our food."

Hunter laughed softly. "They do, especially our bread. They said it reminds them of the bread their women bake when it's still fresh. They've been eating dried meat and stale, hard bread for weeks now."

"I'm happy to hear that. I do remember the bread the Jnaar served us that night by the fires. It was delicious." He rose. "Watch my seat. I'll get myself something to eat," he said before he walked away.

The kitchen in the research station was not as sophisticated as the one on the space station, where one could order a meal from the table, and it would be delivered through a series of conducts to the table, but it was still more advanced than the ones on some other research projects on which he had worked. The menu in the food processor was varied and extensive. He ordered scrambled eggs with ham, a bun, and a cup of coffee by pushing the menu button. After a few minutes, the eggs, the ham, and the bun appeared on a plastic tray in a slot at the end of the counter. He filled his coffee cup from a spout, added milk, grabbed his cutlery from another tray and headed back to his table.

He knew the eggs had never seen a chicken, nor did the ham come from a living pig, but everything tasted the way it should, and the food was nourishing. There were no reasons to complain, but he looked forward to eating some real meat roasted in an oven. The kitchen did have the facilities to do that, because experience had taught planners and researchers to be prepared for the all too real eventuality the automatic kitchen might fail or run out of raw materials for producing food.

He took his place at the table again and started eating, aware of the others watching him. When he looked at their plates he noticed they were empty. "I guess you're all finished eating."

"Sorry about that, sir," Wong said. "Had we known you'd be joining us, we would have waited."

Tennenboum made a dismissing motion with his hand. "That's okay. I guess I should have come earlier." He glanced around the room. "It will be different from now with so many people."

"Our routines will certainly change," Wong agreed. "I'm wondering, sir, how is our food situation? With so many people, how long will the supplies last?"

"We'll be fine until the winter is over, but then we'll have to make it a priority to harvest enough plant material to keep the kitchen going. The meat from that big bird will certainly make a big difference, not to mention we'll be eating real meat for a change."

Hunter snickered. "Everyone will appreciate the change in diet except for Dr. Bonnet."

Tennenboum suppressed the urge to smile. "Yes, there is our Dr. Bonnet. He's not much of a meat eater, being a vegetarian, but we can't worry about the preferences of one man. We have to think of the majority of people."

The alien man spoke at length to Hunter, who nodded and said, "Raaskar is quite impressed with our Station. It reminds him of the caves inside the mountain where he and his clan spend the long winter. Except they don't have such bright lights and the air doesn't smell this clean. He also wants to know when our doctor can have a look at his mate's leg."

"I'll have to speak to our new doctor to find out if she's ready and willing to start working and if she can help this woman."

Tennenboum searched the room and spotted the black woman he had spoken to the night before. He pointed at her table.

"That is the woman who claims to be a doctor. I don't remember her name. As soon as I finish my breakfast, I'll go and talk to her." His eyes locked on Raaskar. "Don't worry, my friend, we'll look after your mate."

The large, purple eyes of the Jnaar were steady as he looked at Tennenboum. When Hunter translated what Tennenboum had said, Raaskar touched his chest. "Stosa."

Tennenboum understood the word, having heard it before. It meant thank you. He smiled. "You're welcome."

Scraping out the last of the eggs, he rose. "Mr. Wong, why don't you take our plates to the recycling bin while Mr. Hunter and our guests talk to the doctor."

Wong nodded and began gathering the plates. Tennenboum made a move with his head in the direction of the table where the black woman sat with a couple other people and started to walk toward the table.

The woman turned her head when Tennenboum approached. He thought she looked younger than he remembered. She stopped eating and tilted her head, looking at him, her brows pulled together. Then her face lit up as she seemed to recognize him.

"Professor Tennenboum, isn't it?"

"Guilty as charged," he said, smiling. "If I remember correctly, you said you were a medical doctor?"

"Yes, that's what I said." Her lips seemed to mock him. "I can repeat it if you want."

He chuckled. "No need. I believe you. I'm afraid I don't remember your name. I apologize for that."

"My name is Cara Mumanba. Dr. Cara Mumanba." She put her hand on the arm of the man sitting beside her. "And this is my husband Kevin."

"Well, I'm happy you're here, Dr. Mumanba. So happy because I may have need for your medical knowledge and abilities." Tennenboum smiled apologetically. "I'm sorry about trying to press you into service already. I know you're all tired from your long trip and need some time to adjust, but this woman…" He indicated the older Jnaar female, who was leaning against the male for support. "She has a leg that has been injured and doesn't seem to heal. We'll need you to look at it and, hopefully, fix it."

It was obvious Cara tried not to stare when her gaze fell on the alien woman, but she couldn't hide her surprise and curiosity. "She's not human," she finally said.

"No, she isn't. None of these three is human. They belong to a race called the Jnaar. Her people have been on this planet for a thousand years," Tennenboum explained.

"A thousand years?" Kevin Mumanba repeated. "Does that mean they're not native to this world?"

"That's what it means. They're strangers here, just like us, but they have adapted." His eyes focused on the Jnaar male. "They're our friends. I promised them help."

"I'll see what I can do," Cara said. "As long as their physiology is like ours I may be able to help her, but no promises."

"Are there others on this planet? I mean indigenous people?" her husband asked.

"Yes, there are. They call their race Sras."

"Are they like us? Have you had contact with them? If so, are they a peaceful race?"

Tennenboum remembered the first contact with the Sras. He remembered Sagela. She had been beautiful, savage, and primitive, but as passionate and wild as a storm in spring. Even though she had been the one to seduce him, fool that he was in his drunken state he had accepted her invitation. Had she been the wife of Uroo, the leader of the tribe, instead of his sister, the first meeting of humans and Sras could have ended in bloodshed and the beginning of a long conflict.

"We've met," he said. "Our meeting was peaceful, but I doubt they are a peaceful race. Neither are the Jnaar. Both these races don't seem to get along. Don't ask me why." He threw a glance at the Jnaar beside him, knowing they would not understand what he said. "The Jnaar and the Sras are not civilized people. Apparently, the ancestors of the Jnaar were, but these are not. They are fierce and live in primitive conditions."

"They don't look fierce," Mumanba said, smiling. "The women are beautiful."

Tennenboum chuckled. "Don't let their appearance fool you. They just arrived yesterday, dressed in furs and nothing else. They survived where we wouldn't. By the way, they don't speak our language."

"How do you communicate?" Cara asked.

"Mr. Hunter speaks and understands their language. He'll act as the translator." He looked at Hunter. "Go with them and Dr. Mumanba to the infirmary and stay there until Dr. Mumanba has determined if she can help this woman and what the procedure will be. Keep me informed."

Hunter nodded. "Understood, sir. What about the Roc meat?"

"I'm sure it'll keep for another day. Start with that task tomorrow."

He left them and headed for the table where he had spotted Cameron and Rockwell. This was as good a time as any to talk to them.

* * * *

As far as Tennenboum could tell, everyone was present in the meeting room. Even his team of researchers. They were all anxious to find out what lay ahead. After speaking with Cameron and Rockwell, he thought it might be a good idea to have an open meeting where the newcomers could talk about their experiences on Nu-Eden and also on the space station and their reasons for coming to the fifth planet. The men and women on the research station would want to know about the situation on Nu-Eden. He was still in a state of dismay and disbelief about the things the two men told him.

According to them, there were no more true humans left on the space station. All of them had been absorbed and re-created by the Xandra, or Great Mother. Her worshippers called her a goddess. The space station was under the control of this alien entity.

Things weren't much different on the fourth planet. They had dubbed it Nu-Eden, but it seemed the paradise had turned into hell. The Xandra ruled over Nu-Eden and had re-created most of the humans on that planet. A few might still be human, but nobody knew for how long.

The ramifications of this were only now beginning to sink into his subconscious. It meant they were stuck here on the fifth planet. There was no returning to the space station. Neither would there be any more communication with anyone on the space station. More important, they would not receive shipments of supplies or spare parts should anything break down. They were on their own.

He only hoped the relief ship from Earth, scheduled to come in four years, would not be delayed or for some political reason or another that would prevent it from coming. Otherwise they'd have to spend the rest of their lives on this planet of ice and snow, not something he wanted to think about.

Perhaps it was a good thing the twenty-two newcomers had decided to escape and come here, looking for sanctuary. It appeared they were prepared to make this new world their home. He wondered how his team of researchers felt about the prospect. This was not an ideal world, but the Jnaar had survived for a thousand years after they were stranded here. He felt confident about the humans' ability to adapt and thrive also.

Humans were a tough species and not easy to eliminate. They would survive.

It had come as a great surprise to hear Rockwell telling him about the aliens they discovered on the space station which the humans had believed was abandoned and dead. According to Rockwell, the aliens had been deep in the bowels of the station, frozen for a thousand years. They called their race Genaar. After they were revived, they told the humans about the evil entity on the fourth planet, but the information had come too late to save the humans from the same fate the Genaar suffered.

Tennenboum knew about the Genaar on the space station from their descendants living on Iceworld, who called their race Jnaar, but he found it hard to believe the aliens had survived that long in the suspended state. Humans did not have the technology to keep anyone alive for such a long time.

The man who was standing in front of the assembled people and talking had introduced himself as Holger Schreiber. His dark eyes flashed with compassion as he talked about his vision of mankind's future on Iceworld. There was something about him that seemed a bit feminine, his gestures and his soft spoken manners, but he spoke well and held his audience captive.

"If we want to thrive on this world, we cannot stay forever hidden in this artificial environment. We have to adapt and learn to use this world's resources. We have to build homes strong enough to withstand the harsh weather, and we have to learn to live on the surface of this planet—our new home."

When he paused, somebody chuckled. "You've only been here one day, Mr. Schreiber, and you know nothing about this planet. Let me tell you about the conditions on the surface. Every season has its own surprises, but the one common denominator they all have are the terrible storms. Who is going to design these homes that can withstand the severe weather conditions?" Tennenboum recognized the nasal voice of Yules Bonnet. He was the meteorologist of the team and knew more about the weather than anyone.

Schreiber favored Bonnet with a little smile. "I will, sir. I'm an architect."

"Well, good luck," Bonnet snorted. "You'll find your abilities to design something useful taxed to the limits of your knowledge and imagination."

"I didn't say it was going to be easy, but we can't give up," Schreiber responded. "From what I heard, these aliens you've discovered managed to survive for a thousand years. Why can't we or our children?"

"Oh sure, we can probably survive, but I don't foresee anyone living and thriving on the surface. We'll have to go underground. The area in this vicinity and, I assume, on much of the planet, is honeycombed with underground caverns and tunnels. That's where I see our future generations living and thriving." Bonnet seemed to shake himself. "Like rats and moles. Not that those tunnels appear inviting to me. The time I spent lost in darkness in those tunnels doesn't make me eager to go back down there."

Tennenboum couldn't agree with him more, remembering the frustrating hours underground searching for Maisoneuve, Yules, and Bonnet, and the confrontation with the monstrous creatures the Jnaar called Dal Losos, the Living Dead Souls.

"You spoke of children, Mr. Schreiber," Rockwell said, rising. His voice dripped with sarcasm. "Are you going to contribute to our gene pool?"

Schreiber's dark eyes seemed to bore into Rockwell's. It was easy to detect the animosity between the two men.

"If need be, yes, I will."

Rockwell laughed. "I thought you didn't like women?"

"I never said that," Schreiber retorted, not hiding his annoyance, "The fact that I'm not attracted to women doesn't mean I hate them."

"Perhaps you don't, but bear with me a little longer. Let me understand this clearly. Even though you're not interested in women, you would sacrifice yourself and have sex with one to keep our gene pool from getting stale, correct?"

"Yes, I would, but I wouldn't exactly call it a sacrifice." Schreiber looked at his audience, the shadow of a smile flickering across his lips, almost like an apologetic gesture.

"I really don't care, but I don't believe you should contribute, Mr. Schreiber. We don't need to taint the genes of our children with your kind of genes."

Tennenboum did not like the direction the conversation was going. He rose and lifted a hand. "Gentlemen," he spoke with a loud voice. "Mr. Schreiber's sexual orientation is not on trial here. Let's keep this civil, please."

Rockwell's chuckle sounded like the growl of a beast. "I'll be civil if Mr. Schreiber promises to forget about adding his abnormal genes to our gene pool." He chuckled again and looked around the room as if searching for a reaction from his audience.

"Abnormal?" Schreiber kept his voice controlled but not his sudden anger. His lips quivered and his eyes burned with cold rage. "Abnormal in whose opinion?" He pointed a finger at Rockwell. "You do not have the right to judge me. Who's to say you're normal?"

"Gentlemen," Tennenboum said sharply. "I must ask you both to sit down. I will not tolerate the exchange of insulting words. Not here on the Station. If we want to live in harmony in these cramped quarters, we need to accept each other the way we are. We cannot afford to do otherwise."

"I'm sorry," Schreiber said. "I'll do my best to fit in and be a useful member of this community." He walked back to his seat and sat down.

Rockwell just grunted and lowered his bulk into his chair.

"We've listened to different accounts now how conditions are on the fourth planet," Tennenboum continued. "It doesn't sound encouraging. I'm sure you'll all agree the colonization of Nu-Eden has failed. Even the space station is lost to us. It appears we are the bastion of humanity in this sector of space. We have to hang on until the relief ship comes to rescue us."

"What if the ship never comes?" a woman asked.

Tennenboum looked at the young woman who had spoken. "That thought has already occurred to me, Miss…?" He smiled. "I'm sorry; I don't remember your name."

"Zyra Frechette." She brushed her blond hair out of her eyes with a delicate hand. "I was working in the research lab on the space station and one of the first to notice that something was wrong with a few of the people. I managed to keep my humanity intact while everyone around me became something not human." Her voice quavered and she put a hand over her eyes for a moment. "I just want to go home."

"So do we all, Miss Frechette. As for the eventuality, the relief ship might not come, that is a remote possibility. Earth will keep on sending exploration ships into space. Our home world is overpopulated and there's no shortage of colonists who want to escape the crowded conditions on Earth. Not many Earth-like planets have been discovered so far, and this star system has been logged and reported. A ship will come, if not in five years, maybe in six or seven. We cannot give up hope. We must stay positive."

Chapter Five

Because he was the only one able to communicate with the Jnaar, Hunter spent much time with the three aliens. He enjoyed their company and it seemed they enjoyed his. Raaskar liked to reminisce about his adventures while hunting wild animals for sport and food in the harsh plains, but he was also interested in hearing Hunter talk about his hunts on other planets. He seemed fascinated by the diversity of ferocious beasts on Hunter's home world Emerald.

Raaskar's mate, Laneea, was also in good spirits. After examining her injured leg, Dr. Mumanba assured her she would get back the full use of her leg and foot. They had to break the leg again, but, with the help of painkillers, the procedure had been painless, and Laneea responded well to antibiotics. Her leg would be as good as new.

Something that might cause problems down the road was that Raaskar's daughter, Raas-ini, seemed to be smitten with Hunter. So far, he had tried to ignore her sometimes too obvious attempts to get his attention, but she was a beautiful and alluring girl, and he found it increasingly difficult to resist her. If her father was aware of the sexual tension it created between Hunter and his daughter, he didn't show it. Of course, Laneea, with a woman's intuition, did not miss her daughter's flirtation with Hunter, but even she did not discourage Raas-ini, and Hunter got the impression she would not mind if Raas-ini and he started a relationship.

It wouldn't be the first time for him to have sex with an alien female. He had not forgotten Arlee, the Sras girl. She had been as fierce as a wild animal in her lovemaking, and he had no doubts Raas-ini would match that fierceness, even though she belonged to a different race. From what he had seen, the Jnaar were no less savage and primitive than the Sras, the indigenous people of this planet.

"Hunter, why are you trying so hard not to be alone with me?"

Raas-ini's sudden appearance and her question startled him. He had not heard her enter the storage room. Stopping his search for a pair of insulated boots he had intended to give to Raaskar as a present, he turned around to look at the Jnaar girl. She stood with her hands on her hips, staring at him with her large purple eyes. It amazed him again how closely related humans and Jnaar really were in their gestures and their manner of speaking. He counted himself fortunate to be able to communicate with them.

"With so many people living on this station it's not easy to be alone, unless you want to spend your time in your sleeping quarters," he responded, fully aware what she hinted at.

"Then why don't you invite me to your sleeping quarters?" She looked around the small room and smiled suddenly. "We are alone now. This is as good a place as any."

"To do what?" he said with a voice gone hoarse.

Her hands touched the magnetic strip of her blouse to open it in the front. He stared at her exposed creamy small breasts and couldn't help but admire their perfect shape. She laughed huskily when she saw his reaction. Coming closer, she took his hand and laid it on one of her breasts.

"Feel them, Hunter. Aren't they soft and warm? You can suck on them if you like. Don't you want to?"

Her breast felt indeed soft under his palm and he suppressed a groan. A sudden pounding in his loins made him realize it had been months since he'd been with a real woman.

"I've seen the want in your eyes when you look at me, Hunter," she purred. "You should know I want you as well." She moved his hand down her body and pressed it into the juncture of her legs. He could feel her puffy mound through the thin material of her pants. "Aren't you curious to find out how it feels to insert your manhood into my belly?" she whispered into his ear.

He pushed her away with an abrupt gesture. "You're a tease, Raas-ini," he said gruffly. "Of course I'm curious. You're a beautiful and attractive girl. I want nothing more than to undress you and take you into my arms. What man wouldn't want that?"

She came close again. Standing in front of him, she searched his face. "Then, why don't you?"

"Because you and I are not of the same species. You're a guest here and will soon move on again. We can't afford to grow fond of each other." He lifted a hand and touched her face. "I don't want any of us to get hurt."

"Why would I get hurt? Do humans hurt each other when they couple?"

He had to laugh. "Not usually. Of course, there are some people who seem to enjoy pain. I'm not one of those. I'm talking about the hurt when two people fall in love and then are forced to part, never to see each other again."

Her smile teased him. "I don't want to fall in love with you, I just want for our bodies to join." Her hand shot out suddenly and touched the bulge in his pants. "You cannot hide your desire for me, Hunter."

Cursing, he reached for her and pulled her slim body against him. Pressing his lips on hers, he kissed her roughly. She returned his kisses with great fervor. Without breaking the kiss, they began to undress each other. In moments, they were naked.

Letting go of her, he stepped back and looked at her, breathing harshly. "Are you sure this is what you want?"

She nodded "Yes, it is." She seemed to study him with great curiosity. "Your whole body is black, not just your face," she observed.

"I was born this way," he chuckled softly, looking over her curvy body. He could see faint, intricate designs of golden threads embedded on her white skin. At first, he thought her body was covered with tattoos, but then he wondered if those patterns might be natural. He also noticed her belly was smooth and lacking a navel.

"Your skin," he said. "Are those designs natural?"

She ran her hands across her breasts and down her belly. I was born with them, just like you with your dark skin. Why don't you touch me and find out how smooth and soft my skin feels."

"Do all the females of the Jnaar have those patterns on their skin?" he asked.

She shook her head. "No. I am different. One of my female ancestors was of the warrior class. I inherited her skin." She stepped up to him and pressed her naked body against his. "Enough talking with our mouths. Let our bodies talk to each other." With that, her long fingers curled around his erection and squeezed gently.

He grabbed her by her slim hips and lifted her. She parted her legs and wrapped them around his torso. Clinging to him, her arms around his neck, she sheathed his hard pole easily and snapped her pelvis back and forth. He cupped her buttocks to keep her from slipping down.

When his legs threatened to buckle, he sank with her to the floor. Their bodies still locked together, he laid her on her back. Her legs opened wide and he moved between her slender thighs with powerful strokes. She squirmed under him and matched every stroke with equal force, slamming into him from below, her breath coming in great gasps and soft mewling sounds escaping her lips.

They moved like two wild animals for a long time. Many times, he reached a point where he thought he couldn't control his urge to end it, but he managed to suppress the desire every time, wanting to prolong the great pleasure she gave him for as long as possible.

She cried out a few times as she experienced an orgasm, quivering in his embrace, her thighs squeezing his hips forcefully, her inner muscles milking him. Then she relaxed with a satisfied sigh, but after a short pause she carried on with renewed vigor.

Finally, the moment arrived when he reached a point of no return. It rushed up from deep inside him, building up to be almost painful.

"Now!" a silent voice said inside his head. Grunting loudly, he pushed deep into Raas-ini's clutching sheath and let it gush out of him. The unbelievable pleasure he experienced was enhanced by the stimulation of the pleasure center in his brain by his invisible companion.

The thought he might get Raas-ini pregnant only rose in his mind for a fleeting moment. He doubted human and Jnaar DNA were compatible.

When it ended, he relaxed into her cradling arms and lay exhausted on top of her, his breath ragged in his dry throat. She crooned soft words and held him tight, her breath warm on his neck.

"You are heavy," she said after a while.

"Sorry," he murmured, pushing up to support his body with his elbows. He looked into her smiling face. "I don't know much about your people and your customs. I hope I didn't break some kind of taboo by putting my seed into you."

She laughed softly. "You didn't. Right now, my body is not in the receptive cycle and our coupling will not produce an egg inside me. Is that what you hoped for?"

"I worried a little it might have disastrous results," he admitted.

"It won't. Besides, I'm not old enough yet to propagate."

"How old are you?"

"I've seen ten winters."

"That makes you twenty in my years. Old enough for anything." He grinned. "Females of my species are highly receptive for getting pregnant at your age. They can produce offspring at a much earlier age, even though it is not recommended."

"How early do they start coupling with a male?"

"Some as soon as they enter puberty and feel the urge, usually with boys of their own age. It is not acceptable in most societies for an adult to have sex with an underage girl. It is still like that on Earth and on the planet where I was born. Of course, the term underage is broad. In some societies, it is not uncommon for a twelve year old girl, six in your years, to marry an older man. It is practiced in most colonies on frontier planets where it is important to increase the population as fast as possible. Where the law forbids it, a man is punished for doing such a thing."

"We do not have such laws. We do not distinguish between old and young. Age doesn't matter when it comes to joining our bodies. We do it to experience pleasure. When a female is in her receptive cycle and wants to have offspring, she will choose a partner and he will fertilize the egg inside her. Her partner can be young or old. An older female may choose a young male if she so wishes."

"Do you choose a partner for life or do you change partners frequently? Your parents seem to have been together for at least as long as you are old."

"They've been together far longer than that. I have three brothers and two sisters. All are older than me. My oldest brother Stasra was hatched almost fifteen winters before I was hatched." She gasped and wiggled her pelvis. "You have grown inside me again."

He grunted when he felt the pulsing of her vagina walls around his hardened member and began moving in and out of her. He froze suddenly when something she'd said surfaced into his awareness.

"Did you say hatched?"

"Yes. Why do you ask?" She milked him gently, making him almost forget his question.

"Are you telling me you lay eggs instead of bearing live young?"

Her movements became more demanding as she slammed her belly against his. She gasped, "Don't stop. I am much more sensitive after a male has spilled his seeds into my vessel."

His feelings of pleasure surged through his system and he moved with vigor atop of her. She seemed like a savage animal, baring her teeth when she experienced her first orgasm. After she calmed down, she panted.

"I want you to take me from the back."

He pulled out and watched her getting to her knees. She turned and presented her buttocks, pushing them up to let him see the puffed lips between her slightly spread thighs. He admired the shape of her round globes and moved behind her. Putting his hard mast between them, he entered her again. She gasped and pushed back against him. Grabbing her hips to steady himself, he fucked her hard and almost furiously until she cried out, her slender body bucking between his hands. He didn't slow down until he exploded inside her with tremendous force. The extreme pleasure of his climax nearly made him lose consciousness.

Cupping her slick body, he struggled to catch his breath, his hands digging into her soft breasts as she still quivered beneath him. "That was some climax," he croaked. "Are all Jnaar women this ferocious in their lovemaking?"

She moved forward and slipped out of his embrace, turned around to lie on her back. Looking up at him with her huge eyes, she laughed throatily. "You haven't experienced anything yet. The third time is even better."

He collapsed beside her. Putting his hand on one of her breasts, he kneaded it gently. "How can it be better?" he murmured. "Besides, I'm done. There's no third time in me." He lay on his side and studied her profile. "You're the most beautiful creature I've ever seen," he said dreamily. "I think I'm in love."

Turning her face to look into his eyes, she smiled. "Weren't you the one who didn't want to grow fond of me? Now you talk about love?"

"That was before I knew what pleasure you're capable of giving a man. You've bewitched me, ensnared me in your net," he murmured. "I'm yours forever."

"We don't live forever," she said, her voice tender and almost sad.

"Not forever then, but as long as I live." His lips curved into a smile. "Since I don't live as long as you, it'll give you a chance to have more lovers after me." He propped himself up on an elbow, his face serious again. "Did I understand correctly when you said you were hatched from an egg?"

"Yes. Why is that so strange?"

"Because humans give birth to live babies. Our women don't lay eggs."

"The Sras do not lay eggs, either. You are like the Sras then."

"Tell me more about your species. I'm interested." He still had one hand on her breast. "If you lay eggs, why do you have breasts? Only mammals have breasts. They're needed to feed the newborn babies with nourishment in the form of milk."

"Our young suckle on our breasts."

"I don't understand. I thought you didn't bear live young."

"We don't. When I'm ready to reproduce, the male I choose will fertilize the egg inside me. Once the egg has grown to a certain size I will deliver it. The egg will be given into the care of the Egg-Guardians to watch over until the child inside is ready to break out of its shell. In the meantime, my breasts will grow larger and my body will produce the life-giving fluid the child needs to survive. That's why I have breasts." She laughed merrily. "Mine don't produce anything now, but they are not useless. I like it when you touch them. It feels nice. You can suckle on them if you want."

He bent over her and took one of her nipples into his mouth. "Like this?"

"Like that." She moaned softly. "Just like that." She stroked his back with gentle hands. "You have hard muscles," she murmured. "You must be very strong."

He didn't answer. Sliding on top of her, he moved between her opening thighs.

* * * *

Hunter didn't think anyone knew about his relationship with Raas-ini, so it came as a complete surprise when Wong spoke to him one morning. "It's none of my business, Irwin, but do you think it's wise to fogg that Jnaar girl? She's an alien and our guest. Perhaps you're taking advantage of her position."

"What the hell are you talking about?" Hunter felt like someone caught committing an illegal act.

"She may be under the impression she has to pay for our hospitality."

"Don't be stupid, Wong. Why would she feel like that? Besides, how do you even know about us?"

Wong grinned. "I've seen you two sneaking into that storage room. Have you forgotten about the cameras in the corridors?"

"Damn!" Hunter cursed. "Anyone else knows?"

"I don't believe so, but I could be wrong. Nobody ever looks at those recordings."

"What's the reason for those cameras anyway?"

"Safety. In case of an emergency, Mother has instant access to all the areas of the station."

"I wish you would stop referring to the master computer as Mother. It's creepy."

Wong's chuckle sounded condescending. "As creepy as you calling that computer strapped to your wrist by your ex-girlfriend's name?"

"That's different. Dawn is an electronic self-aware entity with a personality. The master computer of the station is not self-aware."

"You may think that, but don't be so sure. I've had conversations with her."

Hunter let out an exaggerated sigh. "It, Wong, you've had conversations with it, not her. That computer has no gender, even if it talks with a female voice."

"And your Dawn is a woman? Come on, Hunter. Get a grip on reality."

Hunter didn't answer him. "Dawn, prove him wrong."

A faint mist swirled in front of Hunter. As it became denser it took on the form of a human body. Moments later a young black woman stood between the two men, dressed in a sheer lacy outfit that did nothing to hide her shapely body. She smiled and struck a pose. "Hello, Wong." Her voice sounded soft and silky.

Wong took a step backward and raised a hand, as if warding off some evil spirit. "What the hell are you trying to prove here, Irwin? Why does she appear dressed like that? She's practically naked."

"Meet Dawn," Hunter said, grinning. "She wants to show you how much of a woman she is."

"She's not real, damn it! It's a hologram."

Dawn moved forward, lifted a hand and touched Wong's cheek. Reaching out instinctively, he tried to grab her arm, but his hand met no resistance.

"What the hell! I felt that. How can a hologram feel real?"

"Because I'm not just a hologram. I'm much more than that. In a sense I'm as real as you, except my body is made up of electrical currents instead of physical matter. If you close your eyes and move slowly, you can touch me. You won't be able to tell the difference between me and a woman with a physical body." She laughed seductively. "Go ahead, close your eyes and don't fight me. Just concentrate on your senses."

Making a face, Wong nonetheless followed her instruction. Dawn took his hand and pulled it toward her until it touched her breast. "Close your hand slowly. What do you feel?"

"I feel something soft and pliable," he said. "And warm."

Dawn chuckled. "Open your eyes."

Wong did and pulled back his hand. "I touched your breast," he said. "It felt real. How is that possible?"

"You have a physical body, but you also have a body composed of electrical impulses, just like mine. That's how it becomes possible for us to touch each other." She looked back at Hunter with a mocking smile. "If you ever get lonely and Hunter is willing, he can lend me to you and I can show you what else is possible."

Wong stared at Dawn and then at Hunter. "And you call my relationship with Mother creepy? This, my friend, is more than just creepy, it's…" He threw up his hands. "I don't know what I should call it, but it isn't natural. How does your electronic girlfriend feel about your escapades with the Jnaar girl? Isn't she jealous?"

"I don't get jealous," Dawn said. "There is no reason to be. Whatever Hunter does, I'm always there with him. When he has sex with a female, I experience the same pleasure he does, in fact, I enhance his pleasure."

"This gets weirder and weirder by the minute. Are you telling me you're controlling Hunter's actions, feelings, and emotions?"

"I'm not controlling anything, unless he tells me to do so. I'm only there to give him advice. He has his own feelings, and I have mine."

"You can't have any feelings because you're not real. You're a construct, an artificial intelligence, no matter what you think. A very sophisticated construct but not alive. You can't be."

"You are wrong. I am alive. In a different way, but I am a living entity. I think… I reason… and I feel." Dawn's smile was condescending. "And I am all woman. Perhaps someday I can prove it to you." Her body glimmered and faded away.

"Wow," Wong said, staring at the empty spot where she had been standing just moments before. "I have to admit she looks and acts like a real woman, but this is a little too much for me to swallow. Why have you never told me about this peculiar ability of hers? I've seen and heard you talking to that gadget on your wrist—your invisible companion. I know you call it Dawn, the name of an ex-girlfriend, but this? I had no idea. One of the newcomers, a guy by the name of Rob Cameron has a gadget like this on his wrist, but I don't believe it's anything like yours. How did you manage to keep this a secret?"

"Because of your reaction right now. Professor Tennenboum's reaction was not quite as severe as yours when I told him about Dawn."

"The Professor knows about your relationship with an AI? I'm surprised he didn't lock you up." Wong shook his head. "After meeting her in the flesh, if that's what you can call it, and hearing her talk, I'm not quite certain about your status. Are you still your own man or are you controlled by some alien entity? Because that's exactly what this thing is—an alien entity. How did you come into possession of this gadget?"

"I bought it for a small fortune from somebody who probably was not the legitimate owner. I didn't ask questions. He only told me it was some new, secret technology available only to special branches of the Terran government."

"In other words, this thing is highly illegal."

Hunter shrugged. "Illegal or not, it doesn't matter. We're far away from any law enforcement officials. Besides, I'm using Dawn in the service of the research station, not just for my own amusement. With her help, I learned the language of the Jnaar."

"Still, this whole thing seems unnatural."

"I find it strange hearing you talk this way. You almost worship the master computer of this station. You call the computer Mother and the repair bots and drones cruising inside the walls your children. Now that I find weird." Hunter grinned and gave Wong a sidelong look. "Did you by any chance have sex with Mother? Do you have some secret sex-android stashed away somewhere?"

"Now you're talking crazy, Hunter. You know androids are illegal. When I have sex, I have it with a live woman."

"I've seen you hanging out with Cara lately. I had no idea you two were involved. I thought she was giving it to Kullmann?"

"She is. Actually, she's giving it to about anybody who wants it. Even to Alena Bronsky."

It was common knowledge that Alena was not into men. She preferred women. However, he was surprised to hear that about Cara Gunn, the oversexed love-goddess.

"So how long has this been going on between Cara and you?"

"Perhaps three or four weeks now, but as I told you, I'm not the only one, even though it seems at the moment I'm her number one lover. I have no illusions. It won't last. It never does with Cara as you should know."

Hunter did. She and Hunter had been lovers for a short time, right at the beginning of the research station, until she grew tired of him. He had been hurt, foolishly believing she actually loved him. His feelings for her had been genuine. It took him awhile to get over her, but he had Dawn to console him, even if she wasn't a real human. Dawn filled a void inside his heart and the itch in his pants when he needed it. She never asked because she knew when he needed her.

Now he had Raas-ini, at least for a while. He had no illusions about their relationship. It would end as soon as she and her parents left the station. Unfortunately, as hard as he tried to avoid it, he found himself developing feelings for the alien girl. She was beautiful, gentle, always in a good mood, but ferocious and nearly insatiable in their lovemaking. He knew she would break his heart, but that didn't stop him from searching out her company as often as was possible, which meant every day.

He didn't know if her parents knew about the liaison. Her mother probably did. Daughters can't hide much from their mothers, not when it comes to the matters of the heart.

"Well, you've been trying to get into Cara's pants since she broke up with me. Enjoy her favors as long as she gives them to you," he said to Wong.

"You're not jealous?"

Hunter laughed grimly. "No chance of that. I fogged her for a while and that's it. My feelings for her disappeared a long time ago. My advice is don't give in to your emotions. It's easier that way."

"As long as you follow your own advice with the Jnaar girl. Don't fall in love with her. You two live in different worlds. It'll never work."

"Don't you think I know?" Hunter sighed. "Sadly, it may already be too late. She makes me very happy."

"Just because she makes you happy doesn't mean you're in love. What about that Sras girl, what was her name?"

"Arlee."

"That's right. Arlee. You told me she made you happy."

"It was one night, Wong. One night of wild animal lust, that's all. I have to admit, though, I've been thinking about her a lot. I may have fallen in love with her, too, as strange as it sounds."

"It seems to me you have a streak of weird inside you, Hunter. You seem to fall in love too easily and you're attracted to alien females. First the Sras girl, now the Jnaar girl." His gaze rested on Hunter's wrist. "And let's not forget your creepy relationship with a hologram or whatever that thing is. I'm beginning to worry about you."

"You just worry about your relationship with Mother and those repair drones, Wong. There is nothing normal about that, either."

Wong laughed suddenly. "You're right. You and I, we certainly are a couple of weirdoes. That's why we get along so well." He clapped Hunter on the shoulder. "Come on, my friend, let's go and have a drink together."

Chapter Six

"It seems like such a waste of valuable time sitting in this prison and not being able to do anything." Douglas Roland hunched his thin shoulders. His dark, piercing eyes focused on Cameron. "What's Nu-Eden like?"

Cameron stroked his beard and stared into empty air. "It's a beautiful world with lakes and rivers, jungles, forests, and savannahs. The temperature is pleasant over most of the planet. At night, you can see the stars and three moons that throw triple shadows." He sighed deeply. "It would be an ideal planet were it not for the Xandra."

"What exactly is this Xandra?"

Visions of a beautiful woman with long, red hair and large green eyes kneeling on a giant plant in the middle of a pond rose up in Cameron's mind. She smiled and beckoned for him to join her on the small floating island of purple flowers and broad leaves. He knew it was only a memory he saw, but even here, millions of km between him and her world, he couldn't get her out his mind.

"She's a goddess," he whispered. "A beautiful, alluring goddess."

"An evil entity I gather from what the others say." Roland pursed his lips. "She's the reason you all left Nu-Eden. There's one thing I just can't seem to get my thoughts around. From what I've heard, she killed all the humans and recreated them again. Why didn't anyone get suspicious right at the beginning when the first non-Humans appeared? How did she manage to kill everyone so easily?"

"She has the power to ensnare you with her beauty, to cloud your mind. You can't resist her lure. She appears to you as a beautiful woman and entices you to join her on the plant where she lives. A man is powerless under her spell. While he lies in her arms, lost in the rapture of her passion, she devours his body and then creates him again out of her own body with all his memories intact. Apparently, a man who has thus been created does not even know he has been changed."

"What about the women?"

"The same process, except she appears to them as a handsome man."

Roland gave a little laugh. "What about a lesbian?"

Cameron stared at him, wondering if the man was even taking him seriously. He shrugged. "She probably stays in her female shape. I never thought about it."

"How did you all manage to escape from being changed? There's something else I'm curious about. You said someone who has been changed is not aware it happened? How do you know any of you are still real humans? Are you?"

"Of course I am. My fiancée and I spent most of our time away from Alpha Colony. We stayed at her parents' farm where we had no contact with the Xandra."

"But you spent some time in Alpha Colony, right? I assume that's where most of the colonists on Nu-Eden were located."

"There and in Beta-Colony. I've never been there, but I'm quite certain things were no different there than in Alpha Colony."

"Have you ever met this Xandra?"

Cameron looked into Roland's questioning eyes. "Are you some kind of inquisitor, Dr. Roland? Is that what you do around here?"

Roland's thin lips formed a tight smile. "I'm a geologist like you. At least that's one of my occupations. I can assure you inquisitor is not one of them. I'm a curious individual by nature, and I'm interested in what happened on Nu-Eden. So, tell me, have you met the goddess of Nu-Eden?"

"Yes, I have. The first time I met her I was lost in the jungle. One of her daughters rescued me and guided me back to the colony. I met her again a few times in Alpha Colony."

"Interesting." The lights in the room reflected as tiny dots in Roland's dark eyes. "Did you ever have sex with her and how was it?"

Cameron didn't answer for a moment. "I have," he finally said. "It was incredible. Words cannot describe it. I hope you don't want me to go into details." He smiled. "After all, we don't even know each other yet."

"I don't need to hear any details. I'm not a voyeur." Roland bent forward. "Since you had sex with the Xandra, how do you know you're still a human being?"

Because she told him so. He couldn't tell Roland that. He couldn't tell him what happened to him, either. It was his secret. Nobody must ever know. She had shown him in a vision how he had been attacked and nearly killed by the Honker.

The memory of what she had told him was clear in his mind.

Cameron stared at her. "I do not remember that happening."

"That's because I erased the memory from your mind."

"What else did you do?"

"I repaired your wounds."

"From what I remember I was dead."

"No, not dead, only mortally wounded. You would have died."

"Am I one of your creatures? Is this body not my own?" He was afraid of the answer, but needed to know.

"Much of your body had to be replaced—strands of intestines, damaged organs, and the skin of your belly. One of your legs was destroyed beyond saving, but the rest of you is still the original you."

"What did you do to my brain?"

"You needn't worry. Your brain was still intact and I did not put any suggestions into your mind."

"Why don't I believe you? I know you did something."

An innocent smile played around her full lips. "Maybe just a little. I repaired damaged and not fully functioning nerves and other components inside your body. I also put a tiny piece of myself into you so I could see what you see and hear what you hear."

"You put a transmitter into me?" He almost shouted.

"You could call it that. It's biological and will not cause any harm. I would never do anything to harm you."

She had told him that, but had she told the truth? Was he still wholly human?

"I know I'm human because the Xandra-creatures do not act like true humans. They seem to be happy all the time and prefer sexual intercourse to anything else."

Roland let out a small chuckle. "That doesn't sound so bad to me."

"You don't understand. They seem to have lost the drive that keeps us humans searching out new places and new things. They are nothing but automatons and slaves. None of us wanted to live like that," Cameron said bitterly. "Anything is better than that."

"I'm not sure if living on this planet is so much better. At least on Nu-Eden it was always warm and pleasant. This place... it's a hellhole. The ground outside is frozen and covered with a thick blanket of snow. Wait until you experience your first winter storm. You wouldn't want to be caught outside in that. You'd never survive it. The storms in summer are not much better. You and I we are both geologists, but you can't dig in a frozen ground. You might as well train for a different job. By the way, what is your group's plan for the future?"

"Our plans?" Cameron frowned. "To survive and to settle somewhere pleasant and thrive. There have to be places better than this, further south, perhaps?"

"You may be disappointed. This planet is not an ideal planet for humans."

"Have you explored it?"

"Only the surrounding area," Roland replied. "We don't have a shuttle, only a Landroamer. You can't get far with that."

"Then how do you know there aren't any friendlier and more suitable places? The Sras and the Jnaar live somewhere."

"We don't know much about them. They're primitive people. Even the Jnaar, who apparently came from space, like us, have slipped back into savagery. We've only had contact with them for a short time. As far as we know, they live underground in the winter." Roland's face took on a painful expression. "Do you want to live underground for the rest of your life? Do you want your children to live like... like a bunch of rats?"

"That doesn't sound pleasant." Cameron didn't want to imagine a life like that as his future. To live in semi-darkness, not to see the sun or the stars for months on end, not to be able to breathe fresh air? No, that wasn't his dream. "I still think there are better places where we can build homes suited to the weather here, places that are not so dangerous."

Roland shook his head. "The Jnaar have been here ten centuries, enough time to evolve into a higher society, especially since they came from one. I don't see a great and prosperous future for humans. We're too small of a group. Thirty-seven men and women are not enough to establish a strong society, not under these harsh conditions. Besides, I've no desire to leave the protection of this research station. We can last until the relief ship comes from Earth. I'm going back home in four years."

"What if the ship never comes? Have you given that any thoughts?"

"I've never been a pessimist. I don't let negative thoughts and speculations occupy my mind. If an unforeseen situation should arise, I'll deal with it then. I'm confident the ship will come. Earth needs Lebensraum."

"We left Earth in search of a better life, and none of us has any desire to go back to an overcrowded, polluted world. We'll make that better life on this planet. We have no choice. I feel confident about it," Cameron said with conviction. He wished he did feel confident.

Roland gave Cameron a thoughtful, brooding look. "I and some of my colleagues wandered the underground caves for hours last year. We got lost. It was a scary experience I wouldn't want to repeat. The worst were the creatures we stumbled upon—weird, ugly monsters. Apparently, they're the spawn of some entity that lives in the caves. The Jnaar call the ruler The Dark Goddess. Her worshippers, the Shadow-dwellers, offer her living sacrifices. The Jnaar say she's evil. Strange, this Dark Goddess sounds a lot like your Xandra."

A cold shiver ran down Cameron's spine. He refused to even think of the possibility there could be a connection here. "You're not suggesting these two entities are of the same species, are you?"

"I'm not saying that at all. What I mean is that every planet seems to have some dark and evil power lurking somewhere. On Earth, we have Lucifer, also known as Satan, the devil, or Loki. All primitive societies worship some dark god to whom they make sacrifices. Our legends are full of stories about witches, vampires, werewolves, and other evil creatures. Why shouldn't the natives on this planet or on Nu-Eden be different?"

"Are you saying we made up the Xandra and the danger she represents?"

"I'm not saying that either," Roland replied. "Isn't it possible you've overlooked something? Perhaps the people you thought were changed are still in their own bodies, except some unexplained mysterious power influenced their minds, something like mass-hypnosis. It's possible. This thing about a plant-woman devouring the humans and recreating them seems so far-fetched. It doesn't make much sense and defies all scientific explanation."

"You weren't there, Dr. Roland, but I was. I know what I've experienced. Human women do not secrete sweet nectar from their breasts when you suck on them. Their saliva doesn't taste like honey that gives you incredible stamina. A human woman cannot give you the rapture you would find in the arms of the Xandra or her daughters. You'll never know unless you've experienced it yourself. Yes, it defies all logic and science, but it is the truth."

Roland seemed to have a problem keeping a straight face, but only his lips twitched. "It sounds like a man's wet dream. And you left Paradise behind?"

"It does sound like Paradise, doesn't it? Believe me, it isn't. It's Hell."

"If Hell is like that I am looking forward to dying," Roland said, chuckling. "Somebody told me once I'd be going to Hell because I'm not a religious man."

Cameron laughed, feeling a sudden connection with the other man. "Not only do we have the same occupation, it seems we also share the same philosophy. I guess I'll be seeing you in Hell then. Hopefully not too soon, though." He looked at the device on his wrist, noting the time. "I didn't realize it was getting so late. I promised my fiancée to meet her in the gym."

"That gadget you have there. Hunter's got one similar to yours," Roland observed.

"It's a computer. I use it to log my findings. It is also a communication device and direction finder. Quite useful in the field. I haven't seen Hunter's yet, so I don't know if his is the same one."

"I don't know much about Hunter's, but it is supposed to be quite sophisticated, more than just a mere computer. I heard him talking to it. He's quite fluent in the Jnaar language and can communicate with the Sras. His little device was instrumental in teaching him." Roland's smile was tight. "There is something strange about his relationship with that thing. When he talks to it, you'd think he was talking to a living being. A little bit eerie if you ask me."

"I don't talk to mine," Cameron said, rising. "We should chat again another time. Perhaps you can tell me more about those underground monsters you've encountered."

Chapter Seven

An excerpt from Irwin Hunter's personal log:

It's been nearly three months now since the trio of aliens came to the research station. I've been neglecting my log and only mentioned them briefly a couple of months ago. I didn't know then I would get to know them better than I imagined.

I'm the only one who can communicate with them. I mean truly communicate. I have a good command of their language now, thanks to Dawn and, of course, the opportunity to spend most of my time with them. I don't have much else to do since I'm not a member of the research team. All of them are highly specialized scientists, while I'm a technician. My job as an electrician ended when the station was finished. Wong, with the help of his computer, takes care of the maintenance, which is sort of also a non-job, because there isn't much chance of anything breaking down.

Besides learning to speak and understand their language better, I also got to know all three of them quite well. They are Jnaar. Their people are not native to this planet. They are newcomers, just like us, except they've been here already 1,000 years. The man, his name is Raaskar, is a true hunter and warrior. He loves to tell stories about the hunts he's been on and his clashes with the strange human-like creatures roaming the caves and tunnels that exist underground, but he is also enthralled listening to my stories. When I told him about my home world Emerald, he chuckled and said he wouldn't mind accompanying me there on a hunt. I'm almost inclined to believe he was serious.

Like all the Jnaar women I've met so far, his mate, Laneea, is truly beautiful, as is their daughter, Raas-ini. Laneea is gentle and soft-spoken, but her dark eyes are full of passion. It is almost unbelievable, and one would not guess it by looking at her, but she is already eighty years old. Their race is long-lived. One of the men we met at our first meeting with the Jnaar was 400 years old.

I am smitten with Raas-ini. Her beauty and fierce love-making keeps me under her spell, and I don't want to break it. I crave her constantly. We have sex every night, and it is the best sex I ever had. Perhaps it is all in my mind, but I don't care. I think I really love her and I wish she could spend the rest of my life with me, but I know it's not possible. Our two species are not really compatible. The females of her race lay eggs, like birds or reptiles. I don't believe we could ever have children together. They'll be leaving us soon. Her mother's leg has healed, and Raaskar told me this morning he is ready to move on.

According to him, there is an entrance into the underground tunnels just north of here. Not far from the spot where Regina was abducted. At least now we have an idea how it was possible for her captors to disappear so quickly.

After talking with Professor Tennenboum, we decided to put a small team together to accompany Raaskar and his family into the tunnels and continue our search for Regina. He told us there was a good chance she may still be alive. If any of the Jnaar tribes kidnapped her, they would have had no reason to kill her, even though she was a stranger. If by chance members of his tribe took her, then our search may be over in a short time, and she would be allowed to go home to her people.

Professor Tennenboum assumed without asking me that I would be one of the members of the search team. I didn't argue. It would give me more time with Raas-ini. I have this crazy notion I may be able to persuade her to come back with me after seeing her clan again.

Wong expressed an interest in coming along. Right now, he has the hots for Cara, but he's a realist and knows it will pass. Cara is and will never be a one-man woman. She was born on the asteroid Ceres. Life on the asteroids is different. Their morals and customs are more liberal than anywhere in the Solar System and beyond. It seems staying with one partner for a long time is not one of their customs. I had a scorching affair with her last year, but that didn't last. I'm over her now, but it took a while. I have to admit, even though she grew up in the cold tunnels of Ceres, she's hotter than a solar flare. Unfortunately, a man gets burned easily if he gets too close to her. I did.

The reason Wong wants to be on the team is simple. He really liked Regina, and he hopes if he is part of her rescue team, he will have a good chance to win her heart. I think he's a hopeless romantic, but I like him. We are good friends, and if I could take only one other person along, he would definitely be the one.

I am looking forward to meeting more of Raas-ini's people and to finding out how they really live. Last year I had a chance to go hunting with a group of young Jnaar, and it was quite an experience, especially riding a Heeska, one of those giant birds they use as steeds. It was exciting and exhilarating. Too bad the Jnaar live in caves over the winter. I wonder if there are places on this planet where anyone lives above ground even during the winter months. There have to be such places. Of course, looking outside it seems the whole planet is covered with a thick blanket of snow.

We're lucky to be inside a well-built structure such as the research station, but this little, protective world in which we're living is beginning to get smaller each day. With the newcomers, who arrived here three months ago, our group has grown to thirty-seven people. To be sure, there is enough room in the Station to house a hundred people. We don't even use one of the upper floors, but the rooms are small and we need space to stretch our legs, which means the majority of people will use the common room to spend most of their time. The dining room still has empty tables, and the kitchen is capable of producing more food, but that is not enough.

To see the same faces and to go through the same routine every day is starting to get tedious and depressing. I'm glad I have Raas-ini to spend my time with, and I'm looking forward to leaving this place for a while. Sure, the Station keeps us safe, but it also keeps us imprisoned. I'm ready to break out of this safe shell.

Chapter Eight

Valissa wasn't happy when Cameron told her about his decision to join the small team accompanying the natives into the underground tunnels.

"I don't understand why you have to go, Rob. This missing woman is a stranger to us. She means nothing to you or me. Why risk your life for her? There're plenty of other men who could go instead of you. I'm scared. I don't really know any of these people, and I'll be lonely without you."

Cameron took her face between his hands and kissed her wet cheeks. "I can't explain why I need to go. It's just I have this terrible urge inside me to find out who and what this Dark Goddess is. Apparently, she dwells somewhere in an underground cavern and is worshipped by the Shadow-dwellers. She's the one who created strange, monstrous creatures. If we want to make this planet our home, we need to find out as much as we can about any dangers we may face so we can deal with them."

Valissa's eyes were damp with tears as she looked at him. "How long will you be gone?"

He shrugged. "I don't know. It depends on how long it takes us to find out what happened to the woman who was abducted last year by a group of natives on giant birds."

"These natives, they may not be friendly. You're entering their territory. What if you get attacked by them?"

He chuckled a little. "We have superior weapons, but I wouldn't worry too much. You've met the three natives. They aren't hostile. I've talked to Hunter, Wong, and Dr. Roland. They spent time last year with a large group of Jnaar and found them amiable and friendly."

"What about the real natives, the Sras? And those monsters you mentioned that are apparently roaming the tunnels? I worry about them. What about this Dark Goddess?"

He tried to hide his anxiety, but she knew him too well, and, with a woman's intuition, she sensed something was bothering him. "There's more than you're telling me, Rob. Let's not have any secrets between us. What are you keeping from me?"

He couldn't tell her what the Xandra did to him. She would begin to doubt his humanity. What if this Dark Goddess...

He didn't finish the thought. No! He mustn't even think about the possibility. No reason to get paranoid and drive himself crazy.

Rob planted a quick kiss on her lips. "Just because I don't tell you every thought I have doesn't mean I keep secrets from you, my love."

"So you're keeping things from me by not telling me everything," she said with an accusing and anxious voice.

"Only that there's a chance I may fall in love with one of the Jnaar girls and decide to stay in the tunnels," he said with a smirk. "You have to admit that native girl Raas-ini is very beautiful."

She slapped him on the shoulder. "Oh, you. Always making jokes." She flung her arms around his neck and held him in a tight embrace. "I love you so much. I would just die if anything happened to you. Promise me to be extra careful." She kissed his cheek and leaned back. "Until you leave, you'll have to make love to me every night. I'll wear you out so you won't get any stupid ideas when you meet those native girls."

He grinned. "We have been making love every night. Perhaps that's the reason I want to get away for a while."

"For that remark I may just decide not to make love to you tonight. I'll let you do all the work."

Laughing, he cupped her buttocks and squeezed them. "How could I ever think of having sex with another girl? Who else can move her sexy butt the way you do? You have nothing to worry about. There's nobody else out there."

Liar! Nobody on this planet—not yet, anyway. On Nu-Eden, besides Jirina, Coletta, and Leezi, there were Sister Angela and her whole flock of Angels, Anina McClary, Nurse Mabel, and don't forget the Xandra, and who knows how many of her daughters he had sex with. But they didn't count, because they were before Valissa.

Valissa touched his cheek with a gentle hand. "Just remember that I love you. I'll never be able to love anyone else—ever."

"I know you love me and I love you, too. I will carry that with me. It will help to bring me back to you." Feeling guilty and like a heel, he let go of her.

He needed to forget what happened on Nu-Eden. Much of it had been beyond his control. This was a new planet, a new beginning for both of them. The Xandra was gone and so was her influence over him and his destiny. Gone was the lure of seduction. Whatever happened lay in the past. It must not tarnish his future with Valissa and their life together.

"When will you be leaving?" Valissa asked.

"As soon as possible. The leg of the Jnaar woman has apparently healed enough for her to travel on her own. It also depends on the weather. Even though we'll be transported by the Landroamer to the entrance into the tunnels, the weather has to be stable for us to travel." His eyes searched for the screen in one wall. It displayed the world outside in three dimensions, creating the illusion of a real window. The sky looked gray and he could see a few snowflakes falling. In all likelihood, another storm was coming.

"Will it be cold underground?" Valissa shook herself as if touched by a gust of frigid air.

"According to the Jnaar, it gets warmer the deeper one moves underground. We'll take warm clothing along just in case. Of course, we must travel light, because we'll have to carry everything in our backpacks."

"I wish I could come with you," she said softly.

He was about to say too dangerous, but caught himself. Instead, he smiled. "You would only distract me, sweetheart. You just keep my place warm until I return."

"I'll be cold without you in that bed," she said, pouting and looking at the screen. "I think I'll get rid of the view to the outside and replace it with a picture of gently moving flowers and calm waters."

"Not a bad idea." He looked at the timepiece on his wrist. "How about going for supper? It's almost time."

Most people were already in the dining room. He spotted Malone, Schreiber, and Teresa Hudson sitting at one of the tables and steered

Valissa toward it. Somehow Teresa and Schreiber had formed a friendship, even though Schreiber was sexually not attracted to women, something that didn't seem to bother Teresa. Her two sons sat with the two girls Naomi and Gabriella Lewis a few tables away, chaperoned by Dan Lewis, the father of the girls. The young people seemed to be attracted to each other. It couldn't have worked out any better, because neither of them had much choice when it came to finding a suitable partner.

Malone and Schreiber had been chumming already on Nu-Eden and it was natural they would seek out each other's company, but Cameron had the suspicion that Malone had more than a fleeting interest in Teresa. They'd make a good couple in Cameron's estimation, even though Teresa was probably a few years older than Malone. So far, she hadn't given any indication she might also be interested in him, but she didn't seem to mind his presence at the dinner table.

"We thought you two lovers would not show up tonight." Teresa greeted them with a hearty laugh.

Schreiber, who sat beside her, just smiled and gave Cameron a quick nod. Grinning, Cameron sat down across from Teresa and nodded to the big man to his right.

"How are you, Malone?"

"I'm good," Malone rumbled, got up from his chair, and moved over one seat to make room for Valissa, even though there was still an empty chair between Cameron and Schreiber. His move brought him next to Teresa at the round table.

"You don't look happy," Teresa said, studying Valissa with a little smile. "Trouble in Paradise?"

"Not that kind of trouble." Valissa's face took on a rosy color.

It always surprised Cameron how easily she became embarrassed when people talked openly about sex, or even just hinted at it, but it was also another trait he found attractive about her.

"I just found out Rob's going with the team into the tunnels looking for that woman who was abducted."

"You are?" Schreiber gave Cameron an astonished look. "You don't even know that woman?"

"That's exactly what I told him," Valissa said vehemently.

"It has nothing to do with knowing her or not," Cameron responded, defending his decision. "It's something I need to do. Don't ask me to explain. I don't know the answer myself. Besides, somebody has to go. Apparently, there aren't many volunteers available."

"Who else is going?" Malone asked.

"Wong and Hunter, so far from what I understand. Hunter is an experienced outdoors man. In addition, he was already in the tunnels, so he knows what we can expect. I don't know much about Wong's experience, though, but he and Hunter are friends, which helps."

"Isn't Hunter the black guy with that contraption similar to yours strapped to his wrist?" Teresa's gaze rested on Cameron's arm. "I've never asked you, but what is that thing actually good for?"

"Mine is just a mere computer, invaluable in the field to record and evaluate my findings. I also use it as a direction finder and to communicate with the base back in Alpha Colony. Hunter's gadget...?" Cameron shrugged. "I hear it's something much more sophisticated than mine. Can't tell you more than that because I don't know."

"Why do you carry it with you? You certainly don't need it in here."

"It tells me the time and what day it is." He touched his wrist. "In fact, I already configured it to the local time and also the calendar. You know a twenty-four-hour day on this planet is four point eight hours longer than a day on Earth, the standard we use on all of our ships and even on the space station, don't you?"

"Of course I know that. I've had my timepiece synchronized soon after we arrived here. I may be forty-five, but I'm not senile, young man." Teresa stared at him, pretending to be insulted. "I also know this damn winter is ten months long, and spring another four before we finally have summer."

Her loud laughter made others look at their table.

"You see, I'm not over the hill yet." She glanced at Malone. "There's still plenty of fuel left in this mind and body of mine." She pushed out her chest to emphasize her breasts.

"I never had any doubts about that," Cameron replied. "I'm sure, with that trim body of yours, you can set any man's desires ablaze."

He smirked, remembering how on the day they landed on this planet Teresa had hinted Valissa might have to share him with her and other women.

Her words, reminding him she could still bear children, carried a promise. She certainly wasn't old and definitely an attractive woman. If it ever came to a point he was chosen to father a child with her, he would not find it objectionable. She was a feisty woman and full of passion. Having sex with her promised enjoyment.

He stopped himself from going any further with his train of thoughts, suddenly feeling guilty for even thinking it. He glanced over at Valissa, but she didn't show any reaction to his remark to Teresa. Either she had not paid attention or she decided to ignore it. Most likely the latter. She was quick on picking up these things.

Teresa let out a small sigh. "Thanks for the compliment, Rob, but so far no man has made a move. Too bad you're already taken."

"And I'm not sharing him with anyone," Valissa said, a little bit too sweetly, her hazel eyes doing a quick dart in Cameron's direction.

Clearly, she caught Teresa's invitation.

Malone, who sat in the chair next to Teresa, coughed subtly into his hand. "Perhaps you're not giving the right signals, Mrs. Hudson," he said tactfully.

Teresa rolled her eyes. "What kind of signals does a man expect?"

Malone shrugged his beefy shoulders. "I don't know. Maybe a little encouragement might help."

"Like what?"

Plainly feeling uncomfortable under Teresa's inquiring stare, Malone studied the tattoos on his arms for a moment, obviously groping for the right words. Then he looked at Cameron.

"I've spent much of my time fighting border skirmishes on frontier planets," Malone said. "There was little opportunity to fraternize with real ladies. The women I associated with didn't have any trouble making it clear what they wanted. They also knew I wanted the same thing. I'm not good with words. Maybe you can explain it better to Mrs. Hudson, who clearly is a lady."

Teresa laughed. "Thank you, Mr. Malone. Nothing but compliments for me today. Perhaps not all is lost. You may be surprised to discover what I want, Mr. Malone. In the circles where ladies and gentlemen interact, it's usually the gentleman who makes the first move."

"Then I have much to learn. Perhaps the first thing I need to learn is how to be a gentleman."

"You may possibly need a lady to teach you that, Mr. Malone." Teresa turned her head to look directly into his eyes and smiled. "Is this the kind of signal you waited for?"

"Is it a signal?"

"It's not the first one I've sent you."

Malone seemed to have found the words he had been searching for. "Then I'm a fool for not having noticed them."

"When you sat at our table for the first time, I wondered if I might have kindled your interest, but you never really talked to me directly, so I thought you just joined our little group to talk to Rob." She put her hand casually on his tattooed arm. "My late husband never would have put any tattoos on his body. He thought it was a stupid thing to do. I've always liked tattoos on a man. In fact, I have one on my..." Her smile changed to loud laughter. "Aren't you a little bit curious, Mr. Malone, to find out where it is?"

He grinned, exposing large teeth. "More than curious, Mrs. Hudson."

"Call me Teresa. How are you feeling tonight, Rudi?"

"He's fine," Schreiber said from Teresa's other side. "Can't you see Malone's a bull in heat? I noticed it from the first day he came to sit with us. Now that you've discovered him, does that mean we aren't friends anymore?"

"You'll always be my friend, Holger. I don't have any other girlfriends." Laughing, she patted his hand. "No offence meant."

"Coming from you I know it isn't." Schreiber smiled, obviously not offended by her remark. He probably would have been had anyone else said it, although Schreiber wasn't too concerned what people thought about him being gay. According to his own words back on Nu-Eden, he didn't have strong sexual urges and felt it was a positive thing. He had been unaffected by the Xandra's siren call.

As far as Cameron knew, Schreiber was the only gay man in the group, which, in a way, was unfortunate for Schreiber. In the event they'd have to spend the rest of their lives on this planet, all the men and women would eventually pair off, while he would be left alone.

The couples would have children and become families. They'd be contributing to the continued existence of the human race in their new home, but that didn't mean Schreiber should be considered a useless member of the small human tribe. He was a highly intelligent man with considerable knowledge and could become a teacher to the young children and possibly to some of the adults.

"I might be interested in joining you, Cameron," Malone said. "You said there weren't any volunteers."

Cameron gave the big man an astonished look. "Actually, there aren't any. Why would you want to come along?"

Malone shrugged. "It seems the right thing to do. Probably the same reason I joined the colonization program."

"We've never talked much about our backgrounds, Malone," Cameron said, "I know you've been a mercenary, but that's pretty much all I know about you. You're a tough guy and used to hardships, but what else can you bring to our team that would be useful?"

"I'm good with weapons. You may need a man like me down there."

Cameron chuckled and glanced at Valissa. "I hope we don't have to use any weapons. Hunter speaks both languages, Jnaar and Sras, and will be able to communicate with them. Usually it's lack of communication when strangers begin to quarrel. We'll try to avoid any conflict with anyone we meet. Having the three Jnaar with us will also help. We shouldn't have to worry about the Jnaar."

"But it's always a good idea to be prepared," Malone insisted.

"I can't argue with that."

"What about those monstrous creatures I heard about?"

Cameron heaved a little sigh, knowing Malone wasn't going to leave it alone. He glanced at Valissa. "I've heard about those, but that doesn't mean we'll even run across any."

"How does anyone know this missing woman is still among the living?" Teresa asked.

"We don't," Cameron replied.

"Then why bother going to all the trouble and putting yourself into danger?"

"Because there's always hope."

"From what I've heard about Miss Seagul's disappearance, it seems she was abducted by natives on large birds," Schreiber said. "Apparently, her kidnappers were members of the Jnaar. The Sras don't use those birds.

This information gives us hope she may still be alive."

"As long as there is just a hint of hope she survived, we can't abandon her." Cameron put his hand on Valissa's hand. "If anything like that happened to Valissa, I'd go the end of this world to find her. Hell, I'd spend the rest of my life looking for her."

Valissa squeezed his hand. "I'd do the same for you."

"How touching," Teresa said. "Such devotion, such love. Remember what I told you when we landed on this planet? Don't get too attached. This is a new world. If we want our small group to flourish we have to set aside old customs and morals. I'm afraid there's no room for two people to declare their never-ending love for each other. We must mix and switch partners several times. It's the only way for humans to survive."

"I remember your little talk," Valissa said, her voice carrying a defiant tone. "I can't agree with you. If I should have children from different men, who will produce children with many other women, what is to prevent one of my sons from marrying a girl who may be his half-sister? Wouldn't it be better to have all my children from only one man? In this case, Rob? I wouldn't have to worry my son may marry one of his half-sisters."

"You're correct to a point." Teresa's smile mocked her. "Assuming your Rob keeps his lizard strictly dipping into your fountain and not some other woman's during the months when you're carrying his lovechild."

Valissa threw a look at Rob. "He'd better not," she said vehemently, "or I'll rip it off by its roots."

Teresa let out a loud laugh. Her hand slapped Malone's tattooed arm. "Never fall in love, Rudi. Sex is so much more fun without the burden of being in love."

"I wouldn't be able to tell the difference. I've never been in love," Malone growled.

"I'm sure glad I don't have such problems," Schreiber said.

"Then neither of you know what you're missing," Valissa said. "I love Rob and he loves me. Nothing will come between us to change that."

"What if he meets one of those Jnaar girls when he's underground?" Teresa asked. "I hear all the Jnaar girls are extremely beautiful. The two in our midst are a prime example. Even the mother is a beauty. I hear she's 80 years old."

"That's hard to believe," Schreiber said, looking surprised.

"Apparently, the Jnaar live up to 400 years. They also keep their youthful looks almost till the end of their life." Teresa sighed. "I'm half her age and she looks younger than me."

"You're still a beautiful woman," Malone said.

Teresa smiled and gave him a smoldering look. "Keep this up, Rudi, and you and I will be sharing more than a drink together."

"I may be gay and not an expert on women, but even I can't miss a clear signal like that," Schreiber murmured.

"I heard that." Teresa leaned in his direction and planted a kiss on his cheek. "You're too observant for your own good. Let me tell you something. You may not be an expert on women, my gay friend, but just because you're not into women doesn't mean you don't have to do your civic duty. You have all the necessary equipment. Your services as a stud may be required. You need not be in love to father a child."

"I can't wait for that day to arrive," Schreiber said dryly.

Teresa laughed her hearty laugh. "You may even enjoy it, girlfriend." She punched him in the arm. "All you have to do is close your eyes and pretend you're with another man."

"Why are we even on this subject?" It was obvious Schreiber didn't care for the way the conversation had gone. "I thought we were talking about the rescue mission Cameron is undertaking." His eyes searched out Cameron. "Do you already know when you'll be leaving?"

Cameron shrugged. "As soon as the weather permits us to travel. It may be as soon as a few days from now."

Schreiber nodded. "That's some crazy weather we're having. I'm sure glad whoever designed this Station designed it in such a way not even the fierce storms ravaging this world can destroy it. The shape of an egg is the most logical way to build something like this."

"I guess you should know," Cameron said. "You're the architect. Someday you'll be designing structures suited for the environment of this planet. Perhaps we will be able to live on the surface after all."

"I'm hoping that will happen. I can't picture myself spending the rest of my life roaming dark tunnels below the surface of this world, like a blind mole or some kind of rodent, only to climb out of the darkness into the light and fresh air for a few months in the summer."

"Neither can I." Valissa squeezed Cameron's hand. "I don't envy you for what you'll be doing. Tunnels are not a place where people should live. I hate darkness. I need to see the stars at night and the sun during the day."

Malone smirked and made a sound deep in his throat. "I haven't seen any stars or the sun since we landed. Nothing but thick snowflakes falling from the sky. If this storm doesn't stop soon the Station will be buried under meters of snow and nobody will ever find us."

"I'm afraid there's nobody out there looking for us," Schreiber said. "We're pretty much the only real humans on this forsaken rock."

"I'm not so sure about that." Cameron stroked his beard as he remembered something. "You know, I've had an interesting discussion with Dr. Roland. He told me about a shuttle with a number of scientists on board that went missing a few months after the Station was established. Everyone assumes the shuttle crashed in the mountains. There may be twenty men and women alive and lost somewhere in those mountains."

"If they survived the crash they surely perished in this harsh weather," Teresa objected. "Nobody can live out there."

"Not necessarily. They may have found refuge in caves or perhaps the shuttle itself provided them with shelter. I'm sure they had adequate clothing to brave the cold and enough food rations to sustain them for a long time." Cameron stared into empty air. "On Earth, we've had people living and thriving in the Arctic, living in igloos they built from blocks of snow, eating nothing but raw fish and raw meat. They hunted for their food with primitive weapons, killing ferocious giant bears with clubs and spears. We humans are a tough race and adaptable to our environment."

"Don't forget, it takes generations for a species to adapt," Schreiber said. "To be stranded on an alien planet and thrown into an environment as brutal as this one is a totally different situation. I'm not saying it's impossible to survive in it, but the chances of survival are slim. Perhaps a few really tough individuals may make it, but most will perish." He shook himself and looked at the giant screen displaying the outside world. "I for one would not want to be caught out there. Just looking at those spinning clouds and listening to the howling wind makes me cold."

"I've been to places not much different from this one and endured, but we had the necessary survival gear," Malone said. He exposed his large teeth in a bleak grimace. "I have to admit, even though we always knew we wouldn't be stranded, I wouldn't want to experience those days again."

"I'm glad I'm a woman," Valissa mused. "We don't have the desire to even venture into the unknown. What is it about such places that attract you, Mr. Malone?"

Malone pulled his thick brows into a deep frown. Shaking his head slowly, he said, "Perhaps because I was bored with my mundane life?" His eyes moved sideways to focus on Teresa. "Maybe if there had been a good woman by my side to hold me back, I might not have done the things I've done. I probably would have stayed at home, gotten a steady job, built a house, become a father..." He lifted his hands. "You know—all the things a good husband does."

Valissa's eyes searched out Cameron. "Then why are you not staying home with me?"

Cameron gave her a surprised look. "Please, don't start that again. I'm not traveling to another planet where I will spend years."

"You might as well," she said, her eyes filling with tears. "You're leaving me alone on an alien planet with people I barely know. I just don't have a good feeling about this."

"You won't be alone. There are other women here. You were among strangers on Nu-Eden and you made friends." Cameron suddenly felt guilty, but he had made up his mind about going and he wouldn't change it. Something he couldn't explain drove him. There was a secret hidden in the caves below the surface of this planet and he was determined to discover what it was.

"I'll be your friend," Teresa said.

Valissa wiped the tears from her cheeks. "I appreciate what you are doing, but you and I..." She didn't finish the sentence and shrugged.

Teresa laughed softly. "I know what you're saying. I'm old enough to be your mother, not your friend. How old are you, by the way?"

"I'm twenty," Valissa said, sniffing.

"As old as my son Conrad. My oldest son Sigmund is twenty-two." Teresa gave Valissa a friendly smile. "Just because I'm more than twice your age doesn't mean we can't be friends. I'm not some old woman who should be put to pasture, if you know what I'm talking about. I like to have young people for company. Makes me feel younger. If we can't be close friends, pretend I'm your favorite aunt."

Valissa returned the smile. "I guess I can do that."

Cameron put his arm around Valissa's shoulder. "I'll be back before you know it." He grinned. "They say it's good for a relationship to be apart sometimes. Makes it more exciting when you're together again."

"I think that's a stupid saying. Whoever made that up had some issues with keeping a relationship exciting." She leaned against him. "I'm happy with the excitement we have in our lives. I wish we would never have to be apart."

Cameron didn't miss the thoughtful expression in Teresa's face as she studied him and Valissa. He expected her to make a comment, but she kept silent.

Chapter Nine

The snow came down heavy again. Tennenboum sat in the common room, staring at the large illusionary window that showed only a swirling mass of white and gray. Somebody had turned down the volume of the speakers. The muffled sound from the brutal winds driving the thick snowflakes, barely a soft droning, was audible enough to make everyone realize a terrible storm raged outside. Thick and insulated walls protected the puny humans living inside the giant egg from the freezing cold and destructive force of the winds.

He could almost feel the vibrations running through the wind-assaulted research station, but he knew it was an illusion. It rested safely on massive struts that kept it high above the thick cushion of snow, and nothing short of a nuclear bomb would be capable of rattling or displacing the giant oval structure.

To be caught outside in this wicked weather would be suicide. Even the storms on Centauri IV could not compete with this one, and they had been bad.

"This is the worst one yet," a voice said beside him.

He looked up, squinting at the speaker. He was one of the newcomers to the Station. Even though he wasn't a particularly memorable man who stood out from the rest of them except for being large and beefy, Tennenboum remembered his name.

"Mr. Malone. What's on your mind?"

The big man took the seat across from Tennenboum. Rubbing a broad hand across his bald head, he cleared his throat. "We've been here now for ninety days or so, Professor. I'm losing count. All I know is I'm going a little stir-crazy." He smiled, baring large teeth. "I heard you're looking for a volunteer to join the group that will accompany the three natives into the underground tunnels. I wouldn't mind going with them."

"Why?"

"Like I said, I'm getting restless. A little action might do me some good."

"You may get more than just a little action. Have you ever spent time inside dark tunnels, Mr. Malone?"

Malone nodded. "I'm a mercenary. I've been to many dark places, one of them the mines on Akrilla, the seventh planet in the Gamma system. You've heard of it?"

"I have. I had a colleague, a geophysicist like me, who went there with a research team. Never came back. He died in those mines." Tennenboum shook off the bad memories trying to darken his mood. Gord Carpenter had been more than just a colleague. They spent three years together on Devil's Nest. He was still alive because of Gord.

"Sorry to hear about your colleague. Then you're aware that Akrilla is one of the most dangerous planets we've discovered so far."

"So far, but there will be others." Tennenboum allowed himself a dour smile. "I see no problem with you joining the team. Have you spoken to any of them about your plan?"

"I've mentioned it to Cameron. He knows me. His brother Ted and I used to be friends."

"I wasn't aware Cameron had a brother. What happened to him?"

"He was mortally wounded when we grabbed much needed supplies from the space station. We had to leave him behind. He's probable one of the Xandra's creatures now," Malone said with a bitter voice. "Cameron took it pretty hard. He doesn't want to talk about it."

"I can't say I blame him. It's always difficult to lose someone you love," Tennenboum agreed. "Sometimes it's best not to remember." He studied the big man across from him. "I don't know what you'll find in those tunnels. If anything happens to you in there, you'll be on your own. Don't expect any help from us. There will be no communication either. I won't even try to guess how long you'll be down there."

Malone lifted his beefy shoulders. "What's the difference? To be stuck inside these prison walls or walking inside a long tunnel? At least I'll be able to stretch my legs."

"Did you discuss it with anyone else?"

"I've talked some with Hunter. He told me about those ugly half-dead creatures we may encounter." He grinned. "That won't bother me at all. It'll be fun blasting some of them."

"I'm certain you'll get a chance to do that," Tennenboum said, wondering if Malone was a man who took orders easily or if he had a streak of rebel inside him.

Malone reminded him quite a bit of Professor Maisoneuve, who was not easy to get along with either. Ever since they got to know each other better, their relationship was not as strained as it was in the beginning. He hoped Malone would not cause trouble for the rest of the team.

"So what's your verdict?" Malone said, pushing his bald head a little forward, giving the impression of a bulldog waiting for his master to throw him a stick to fetch. "Do I have your blessing?"

Tennenboum leaned back in his seat. "If that's what you want, I'm not holding you back. As long as the other men have no objections, I have none either. You'll be relying on each other for survival and it's important you mesh with them."

"I'm easy to get along with, Professor," Malone assured him. "I adapt quickly." He smiled. "That's why I'm still alive."

"You'll have to wait until the storm dies down." Tennenboum pointed at the screen. "It can last for days still, but be ready when it happens. You may only have a short time. Right now we're in the middle of winter and the storms come more frequently it seems, and they're getting worse. You'll probably have better weather underground." He chuckled. "Perhaps going underground is not such a bad idea. If I weren't the head of this research station, I might even join you." He sighed. "Sometimes it's better to be at the low end of the totem pole than at the top. Too many responsibilities and too little fun."

"Well, then I'm glad I'm at the low end," Malone said, rising from his seat. He tipped his hand against his temple in a quick salute. "I'll be talking to you again before we leave, Professor."

Tennenboum watched him walking away toward the bar at the end of the common room, probably to talk to Wong. He saw him sitting on one of the stools. Wong was the other member of the team going underground. Tennenboum didn't want too many people leaving the Station. It would be best to send a small team. So far there were only Hunter, Wong, and Cameron. Malone would be the fourth member. Actually, he didn't want anyone else going. There was no reason to send an army into the tunnels to search for one person. Should anything go wrong, to lose another four people would be tragedy enough.

His gaze wandered to one of the tables nearby and rested on the woman sitting at it by herself, nursing a drink. She had a narrow face with classic lines. Her thick, black hair curled around her slim shoulders.

She saw him looking and gave him a friendly smile. He nodded and smiled back. Picking up her glass, she got up and came walking toward his table. The skirt she wore clung to her shapely figure. Its hem stopped just above her knees, revealing a pair of nice legs.

"I hope I'm not intruding, Professor Tennenboum, but you seem to be alone and lonesome. May I join you at your table?" Without waiting for an answer she sat down.

She bent forward and reached across the table, holding out her hand. The top button of her blouse was undone, giving him a good glimpse of her creamy breasts as her blouse fell open. He noticed the lack of a bra when he saw her breasts swinging freely in front of his eyes.

"I'm Claudette Lavallee. I don't know if you remember me. We haven't actually had much of a chance to talk."

He took her hand into his and held it for a moment. It felt warm and soft. "I remember you, Mrs. Lavallee, but you're right, we haven't talked much. I apologize."

Her laugh sounded amused. "No need for an apology, Professor. Call me Claudette. I hate to be called by my last name."

She removed her hand and picked up her glass. Lifting it to her lips, she sipped from it. Her dark eyes looked at him over the rim as she drank. Putting it down, empty, she smiled.

"I should stop drinking, but now that I've got a chance to talk with you, perhaps I'll have another one." She looked around, obviously searching for one of the two girls who were on serving duty. When she spotted her, she waved and called to her. "Gabriella, be a good girl and bring me another drink. Don't spare the alcohol." The young girl nodded and hurried off to get the drink.

"I wish I had a daughter like that," she said with a low voice.

"You don't have any children?" Tennenboum said.

She shook her head. "My husband and I decided it was for the best, considering our relationship."

"I don't understand."

"You can't produce children if you don't have sex," she said bluntly.

Her directness slightly embarrassed him. "Is it a medical problem?"

"I almost wish it was." She stared into her empty glass. "It happened about a year after we got married. I caught him having sex with my younger sister. She wasn't even old enough yet. Then he had the nerve to say it wasn't his fault. She seduced him and he couldn't resist. No guts, that's what it is. He's got no guts to admit he was wrong. I haven't let him touch me since that day. He broke my trust in him and his promise to be faithful, something I can't ever forgive him. Something I will never forgive."

Tennenboum didn't know what to say and sipped from his own drink. It was warm and tasted stale.

"Would you forgive your wife for cheating on you? With your younger brother?" Her eyes were wide open as she stared at him.

"I'm not married. Never have been. I don't have a younger brother, either. A couple of sisters, but I guess that doesn't count." He smiled.

The girl came with the drink and set it down in front of Claudette. She took it and emptied half of it. "Pretend you're married to a cheating wife and pretend you have a brother. Would you forgive them?"

"I don't know, Claudette. How can I answer that truthfully? I'm not a man who carries grudges for long, but having my wife, my imaginary wife, cheat with another man might be something I could not forgive, either."

"Where you ever in love, Professor?"

Oh, yes. He had been in love. It was so long ago and yet, the memory of Elisa would never leave him. Could what she did be considered cheating? She promised to wait for him but didn't. He had forgiven her, but the pain was still there.

"I was in love," he said slowly. "When I was young."

"What happened?"

"She married another man."

"I should have married another man," Claudette said. "Perhaps I would be happy now." She laughed without humor. "At least I would have regular sex. I'm not a cold lump of ice. I crave the attention of a man. My body longs for hot and sweaty sex."

Tennenboum cleared his throat to hide his uneasiness. "Not all of us are so lucky," he murmured.

Emptying her glass, she slammed it on the tabletop with a little too much force. "You could get lucky tonight, Professor," she said, her words coming out slurred. Then she put her hand over her mouth and giggled like a young girl. "I think I shouldn't have had this last drink. I've consumed too much alcohol already and it loosens my tongue. I'm not usually this forward, Professor Tennenboum. We're not even on first name basis yet. What is your first name, anyway?"

"Martin. My friends used to call me Marty." He didn't remember the last time somebody called him by his first name.

"Marty." Her red lips formed a wicked smile. "I'll call you Marty. I want to be your friend, Marty." She pointed a finger at him. "I like you, Marty."

He looked around at the other tables to see if anyone was watching, but it seemed nobody was paying attention to him or the woman. "I think you are right. You've had too much to drink, Claudette. Besides, it's getting late. You should sleep it off. You'll feel better in the morning."

"Okay." Getting to her feet, she stood, swaying a little. "On second thought, I think I need your assistance. I may get lost or pass out on the way to my room."

He took her elbow and led her out of the dining room. As they walked down the corridor, she suddenly stopped walking.

"What is it?" he asked, a little concerned about her state.

She stepped in front of him and put her arms around his neck. "Did I tell you that I like you, Marty?" Her dark eyes searched his face. "I really do, you know, because you listened to me."

Feeling uncomfortable standing in the corridor like that, he sought to distract her. "You told me so. I like you, too, but we should get you to your room."

She pulled her brows into a frown. "I don't really want to go to my room."

"Where do you want to go instead?"

"To your room, Marty. I want you to make love to me. Sweet and passionate love." She lifted up her face to kiss him on the lips.

Even though her lips were warm and pliable on his, he didn't respond. He pushed her gently away. "You're drunk, Claudette. You don't know what you're saying."

"I know exactly what I'm saying. I'm horny and starved for a man's attention." She pressed her body against his and kissed him again, more demanding and with more passion.

Unable to stop his body from reacting to her nearness and her fervor, he returned her kiss. His arms went around her slim form and held her tight. She felt good in his arms. Chuckling into his mouth, she pushed her lower body forward with a slow grind.

His hard penis pressed into her belly. She released him and gasped. "This tells me you want me too." Slipping from his embrace, she grabbed his hand and pulled him with her. "Come on. Let's not waste any more time."

Following her somewhat reluctantly, but with growing excitement and eagerness he let her lead him down the corridor. They arrived in front of the door leading into his quarters.

"How did you know where my apartment was located?"

She smiled mysteriously. "It wasn't difficult to find that out. Now, let's get inside." Somehow, she didn't sound so drunk anymore, but he didn't give it much consideration. His desire for her damped out any rational thought.

He ran his hand over the key plate. When the door slid open, he let her enter first. The door slid shut behind him and he locked it with a quick verbal command. Claudette was in his arms the moment he turned around. Her hands were already busy opening his belt. His pants slid past his hips. She pushed down his underwear and sheathed his erection with her hand.

"This feels nice," she murmured. "I haven't had the pleasure of holding a man's hard organ in my hand since before I went into deepfreeze five years ago."

He groaned and crushed her to him, kissing her roughly and then releasing her. "Take off your clothes. I want you naked," he rasped,

Stepping back, she laughed, and opened her blouse with slow fingers, watching him with lowered lids. "Even though I want you badly, there's no hurry anymore," she said in a sultry voice. "We're alone now. I want you to drool and lust for me. It enhances the pleasure for both of us."

Her naked breasts tumbled out as she peeled off her blouse. He let out a little moan when he saw their perfect shape. The only time he had the pleasure of looking at a woman's nude body since he left Earth was when he watched Cara Gunn swimming in the lake, and the last time his hands touched a woman's breasts was months ago, when he had sex with Antje Swornson, and before that with Sagela, the Sras female.

Claudette pushed her skirt down past her hips and let it pool around her feet. Then she hooked her fingers into the top of her lacey panties and slid them down slowly. Lifting her legs, she pulled first one and then the other leg out of her panties, and then she stood completely naked in front of him.

"You're still dressed." She pouted in a delightful way.

"I've been mesmerized by your lovely body," he said in a hoarse whisper.

He drank in the sight of her solid trim figure, realizing how much he ached for a woman's loving touch, for the intimacy of feeling her warm body in his arms, and for the moment of ecstasy when their bodies joined in sexual union. He yearned to see her desire for him in her eyes, and to watch her face as she experienced the joy of an orgasm.

Laughing with obvious pleasure, she did a slow turn, showing off her full buttocks and the curve of her slim back. "It's been a long time since a man admired my body and gave me a compliment," she said, her eyes large and full of promise. "You are a true gentleman, Martin Tennenboum." She walked up to him and finished opening his shirt. She slipped it off his shoulders.

"Better step out of your pants. I don't want you tripping and breaking something."

When he was naked, she moved against him and trapped his erect member between her strong thighs. "Nice," she said, her breath catching in her throat. Moving her lower body back and forth, she rubbed her slit over his mast.

He grunted and put his hands on her buttocks. Her pussy felt wet on his penis and he knew she was ready. Gathering her into his arms, he carried her to his bed and laid her down. She looked up at him expectantly, her lips open, her breath coming in little gasps of anticipation. He lay on top of her and slid between her inviting, opening thighs. When he penetrated her, she let out a cry of joy and pushed against him. She was wet and soft, and he moved between her spread legs with slow, measured strokes, pushing ever deeper into her clutching, hot love-channel.

It didn't take long before she began to whimper and shudder beneath him as a powerful orgasm shook her body. "Oh... oh..." she cried out, moving her head from side to side, "...this is heaven... don't stop... please, don't stop..." Her fingers raked his back, her hips slammed into his.

Jubilant and exhilarated, he tried to keep his own climax at bay for as long as he could, but he had been without a woman too long, much too long. His hunger overwhelmed him and he surrendered to the strong desire. It built deep within, rising to the surface with the force of a tornado. The pleasure was almost painful as he ejaculated inside her clutching vessel. He shouted his own joy, lay jerking like a rabbit between her widespread thighs until it was over. Then he lay in the circle of her arms and thighs, exhausted but elated, gulping for air, his heart pumping in his chest.

Holding him tight, she whispered into his ear. "Thank you for not rejecting and embarrassing me, Marty. I'd forgotten the pleasure it brings to feel a man's penis pumping inside me, to feel his hot sperm shooting into me. That was wonderful." She kissed him gently and stroked his back with soft hands.

"You made it wonderful," he said, his breath still coming in great gasps.

She chuckled and wriggled her lower body, her tight sheath contracting around his semi-erect member. "I admit I did help a little, but this big feller gave me all the pleasure. I wish we could coax him back to life."

He pulled out of her and rolled onto his back. Cupping one of her breasts with his hand, he massaged it gently. "If we give him a little rest, maybe he'll rise again, and if you'll invite him for another visit, perhaps you can feel him pumping one more time."

She laughed. "You have a pleasant sense of humor. If you let me stay the night, I'll let him visit as often as he wants. I'm far from done."

Chapter Ten

It finally stopped snowing. Even though the wind still blew from the north, it was a slight breeze compared to the terrible force it had displayed only days ago.

Looking out of the Landroamer's window, Hunter could almost find a certain beauty in the white landscape. The mountains lay behind a foggy haze in the distance and the sky was covered by swirling clouds.

"Looks like it's going to snow again quite soon," Malone observed from the seat behind him.

"We'll be underground by then." Hunter turned his head to look at the big man.

Given his preference, Hunter would have liked to see Wong as part of the team, but Professor Tennenboum decided at the last moment to keep at least one man who knew how the Station worked. Since Wong had been the one to install the master computer, he was the logical choice.

Malone was a mercenary, a soldier for hire, an expert when it came to weapons. Hunter didn't know how important that would be, but, according to Tennenboum, the big man had been to a few different planets and endured plenty of hardship in hostile environments.

The third man of the team, Cameron, was a geologist, used to spending time outdoors and living under primitive conditions. That was important. It wasn't going to be a picnic traveling through dark, possibly damp tunnels, sleeping on the hard ground, eating rations, and drinking stale water.

The other passengers in the Landroamer were the three Jnaar. Raaskar, Laneea, and Raas-ini. Hunter had managed to persuade them to leave their sled behind. It was much easier and faster to travel with the

Landroamer to the entrance into the tunnels. Their few meager belongings could be carried in the backpacks Professor Tennenboum gave them, along with canteens for their water and food rations. Raaskar had gratefully accepted the hunting knife, but declined to take one of the offered laser rifles. He preferred his bow and arrows to hunt for food and to defend himself against his enemies.

The Landroamer skirted the forested area north of the Station, heading for the mountains to the east.

"This must be the place where Regina was captured." Alena Bronsky, who drove the Landroamer, pointed toward a grove of trees sticking out of the deep snow. "There's a pond and a creek under all this snow. It's frozen now, of course."

"How do you know about the pond?" Cameron asked.

"I was among the search team looking for Regina," she explained.

"Even judging by the trees it's difficult to tell how deep the snow really is," Malone said.

"The blanket of snow is at least three meters thick." Hunter guessed at the depth of the snow cover but he was quite certain his estimation was close. Had it not been for the magnetic cushion the Landroamer floated on, they would have had a difficult time traveling across the snow.

Alena followed Hunter's instructions as to which direction to travel. Raaskar coached him and he translated the information. He was still the only one who spoke the Jnaar language fluently, even though Cameron had made some progress with the help of the computer strapped to his wrist.

Hunter had been a bit surprised when he saw the computer on the geologist's wrist and wondered how sophisticated it was. As far as he knew, not many owned gadgets like that because they were expensive and mainly used by government officials and law enforcement agents. Cameron informed him that his device could not compare to Hunter's. Dawn was an AI and self-aware, while Cameron's device was nothing but a simple computer without any awareness of its existence.

It could not interface with its owner the way Dawn did. Hunter learned by having Dawn's artificial mind merge with his and becoming one with the AI. Cameron could only connect to his computer via a tiny device inserted into his ear. The computer would teach him subliminally while he slept, which was not nearly as efficient as the way Dawn taught him.

Of course, there were many other things Dawn was capable of doing, things a regular computer could not accomplish. Dawn was Hunter's invisible companion; Cameron's gadget was basically nothing but a sophisticated electronic adding machine.

The surrounding area changed slowly from a wooded landscape to rugged rocks rising out of the snow. In the not so far distance they could see the sheer wall of a cliff signaling the end of the valley and the start of the mountains.

It took almost another hour before Raaskar advised Hunter to be on the lookout for a particular outcropping of rock. Hunter translated it to the others, but it was Raaskar, who called, "Stop!" after about ten minutes of searching.

Alena brought the Landroamer to a halt. The vehicle settled onto the snow to allow the passengers to disembark. After slipping into his insulated suit and strapping on his snowshoes, Hunter was the first one to climb out. The snow was still quite soft from the recent snowfall, but his webbed shoes only sank in a few centimeters. It took him a moment to adjust to the frigid breeze assaulting his unprotected face. After breathing the warm air inside the Station and the Landroamer, it came almost as a shock to his system. Pulling a pair of gloves out of his jacket's pockets, he slipped his freezing hands into them.

Then he stepped away from the vehicle to make room for the others. One by one they joined him outside.

"I'm not coming out," Alena informed them over the outside speakers. "I'll unlock the cargo door for you."

Hunter gave her the okay-sign and went to the back of the Landroamer. The door to the cargo compartment opened and he removed his backpack, utility belt, and his laser rifle.

Malone took out his stuff next. He hefted the laser rifle with one hand. "I hope we don't run into any trouble, but if we do, I won't regret the extra burden I have to carry with this piece of hardware." He pulled the hood from his jacket over his bald head. "Damn cold," he cursed. "I hope it's warmer in the tunnels."

The three Jnaar removed their gear from the storage compartment. All three of them were dressed in their own furs and clothing, even their leather boots. They didn't trust the flimsy looking garb and footwear the humans wore. Raaskar slipped on the straps of his new backpack. Then he slung his quiver filled with arrows across his shoulder and grabbed his bow. Laneea and Raas-ini carried spears. Primitive weapons, but Hunter knew in capable hands they were as deadly as a sophisticated laser rifle, especially in close quarters.

"I'll wait until you give me the signal," Alena said again over the speakers.

Hunter lifted his arm in a farewell gesture and turned to Raaskar. "Which way?"

Raaskar pointed to a grouping of tall rocks. "Over there."

"Let's go." Hunter began moving in the indicated direction. Even with his snowshoes, it was not easy walking on the soft snow, mainly because he was not used to this mode of travel. It was a good thing they didn't have to go far. Glancing over at the three Jnaar and the apparent ease they displayed walking on the snow with their own version of snowshoes, his respect for the aliens rose, remembering they had traveled many kilometers pulling a sled behind them when they arrived at the Station.

It took them nearly ten minutes to reach the rocks. They grew taller as they approached and loomed over the travelers. Hunter let Raaskar take the lead, following him with a minimal amount of caution. Even though he didn't expect any trouble, his years of stalking dangerous animals on his home planet Emerald had taught him caution when in unfamiliar territory.

Moving around the massive rock formation, they found a natural bridge covering a large area between the tall rocks and the cliff wall. The snow had drifted under the bridge.

"In there," Raaskar said. He began climbing, followed by his mate.

Raas-ini, who hadn't spoken to Hunter since they entered the Landroamer, waited for him, smiling. "Soon you will be in my world, Hunter. It is much different from yours."

"I won't be worried if I have you and your father as my guides," Hunter said, smiling.

She nodded and followed Raaskar and her mother into the twilight under the bridge. Hunter turned to his companions. "Go ahead. I'll be with you in a moment." He spoke into the gadget on his wrist. "Alena. This is Hunter. We found the entrance. We'll be on our way."

"Okay. I'll be leaving. Good luck and come back safely." Alena's soft voice seemed to be coming from somewhere in front of him, but Hunter knew it was the way Dawn transmitted the incoming message.

"We will. You take care too." His gaze traveled across the expanse of the snow-covered landscape, back toward the forest and then, with a last look at the clouds, he realized it might be quite some time until he would see them again. The world he was entering was dark and small. He'd be traversing narrow tunnels with walls on each side and a ceiling close enough to touch. He hoped he and his companions were up to the task. There was a vast difference between spending weeks, perhaps months, in such an environment instead of only a couple of days and nights. It would be a long time without seeing the sun or the open space of this valley he'd been looking at for this past year.

Cameron and Malone had already disappeared into the semidarkness as he hurried to catch up with them. Climbing the gradual incline, his eyes adjusted to the dim light and he saw the others standing in front of a dark hole in the cliff.

"We feared you changed your mind about coming with us," Cameron said as Hunter closed the gap between him and his companions.

"No chance of that," Hunter assured them. "I just had a moment of nostalgia, that's all."

There was no snow anymore on the floor, which made walking with his snowshoes difficult. When he bent to undo them, he noticed the others had already removed theirs.

"What should we do with them?" Malone said, dangling his in one hand.

"I don't believe we need them in the tunnels," Hunter replied, looking around for a place to hide them. While he searched, he concluded they could leave them just about anywhere. There was nobody around to steal them. He spotted a crack in the wall and pointed at it.

"We can leave them over there. They'll be easy to find when we come back."

Cameron and Malone handed him theirs. He took them and carried all three pairs to the crack. It turned out to be more than just a crack. More like a tiny cave, large enough to hide more than just their snowshoes. When he stashed them inside the cave, he heard footsteps behind him and turned. It was Raaskar.

"I will leave ours with yours," the Jnaar told him. He gave a little chuckle. "I can always make new ones."

Hunter grinned. "I hope we don't need any where we're going."

"No. You won't. There is no snow underground." He pointed at Hunter's insulated suit. "You won't need that one either. It will be warm."

"It's still cold out here," Hunter said.

"Yes, but it won't be for long. We will find a place to hide them once we are in the tunnel." Raaskar turned to walk back to the others. "Now we begin the journey home to my people."

The tunnel they entered was dark. The humans switched on their headlamps lest they stumbled into a wall or tripped over an obstruction on the floor.

"How long do these things last?" Malone asked.

"About a hundred hours, maybe more," Hunter replied.

"I've got a dozen spare power packs with me," Malone said. "That'll supply me with over 12,000 hours, which means about a hundred days if I use my lamp for twelve hours a day. I assume you two have the same amount of spare power packs. That'll give us over three hundred days if we use one lamp at a time. Should be enough for us to get back home."

"Your math sounds logical, but don't forget, we may need light for more than twelve hours a day. We won't be sleeping for twelve hours," Cameron corrected him.

"My math is close enough. I suggest we use only one lamp from now on. I don't feel like being trapped in the darkness of these tunnels," Malone said.

"Neither do I," Hunter responded, echoing his concern. "This happened to Dr. Roland, Dr. Bonnet, and Professor Maisoneuve last year. Their torches went out while they were exploring the tunnels. They had no spare power packs and nearly perished. We can't treat this lightly." He turned to Raaskar. "How do you travel in these dark tunnels? You don't have portable lights the way we have."

Raaskar chuckled. "It would be nice to have such lights, but we don't really need any. We can see quite well with the help of the glow-roots that grow naturally on the walls and the fire-rocks in the ceiling."

"I don't see any," Hunter said, looking around.

"You will see them when you turn off your lights."

They switched off their headlamps. At first, Hunter saw only darkness, but as his eyes adjusted, he could make out faint glowing points in the walls and the ceiling above them.

"That's not very much light," he observed. "I can barely see my hands in front of my eyes."

"The roots and rocks will get brighter as you travel deeper into the tunnels, but even now everything is clear to me. Why not to you?" Raaskar sounded surprised. "It just occurred to me that there may be a difference in our eyes. Your eyes are much smaller than mine. Perhaps, we can see a broader spectrum than you."

"I never thought of that, but it makes sense. It may also be because your species has lived in darkness for so long that your body and senses adapted to your environment," Hunter suggested.

"That maybe the case," Raaskar agreed. "If you feel more comfortable you may use your lights."

Hunter switched on his headlamp, flooding the area in front of him with its bright light. "Much better," he said. "Now, shall we get going?"

The tunnel seemed to lead straight ahead, but after walking for about fifteen minutes it made a sharp turn and Hunter noticed a distinct decline. He was also feeling warm inside his suit. After about another thirty minutes, he stopped walking. "I'm getting hot," he said. "I don't know about you gentlemen, but I'm taking off my suit."

"I thought you'd never make that suggestion," Malone wiped his face. He had flipped back his hood the moment they entered the tunnel. "I'm dying inside this damned suit."

"I second that," Cameron said, already stripping off his.

"We should have left them back where we stashed the snowshoes," Malone said. "We wouldn't have frozen to death from the short walk into the tunnel."

"Hindsight," Hunter said, looking around for a good hiding place.

Cameron had done the same thing. He seemed to have found a suitable spot high up on a shelf. There was a hole in the wall right under the shelf. "We can stuff them in there," he said, pointing.

"Good enough," Hunter said and headed for the hole, carrying his suit.

A loud, guttural cry from behind him made him stop and look back. He saw Raaskar charging at him, one of the spears clutched in both hands. Expecting to be run through and wishing he hadn't put his laser on the ground when he took off his suit, he fell into a combat stance, but Raaskar rushed past him, letting out another harsh yell. A loud roar made Hunter swing around to witness Raaskar plunging his spear into the thick body of a snakelike creature with a grotesque head and an open maw filled with long teeth. Part of the creature's long body was still hidden inside the hole Hunter had been heading for.

Before he could assess the situation, another person swept by him and thrust a spear between the snapping jaws. He recognized Laneea. She screamed a high-pitched sound that could have frozen a charging Keeras in its tracks as she stabbed the spear a second time deep into the gullet of the roaring creature. A stream of some dark liquid gushed from the oral cavity and the beast emitted a gurgling sound, swinging its large head back and forth, trying to dislodge the weapon, but Laneea persisted.

Raaskar yanked out his spear and handed it back to his daughter, who had come to his side. Then he moved closer to the undulating head. Using his newly acquired hunting knife, he began hacking at the long neck. Blood jetted from the wound, covering Raaskar's bare arms, but he kept on hacking. Soon the creature stopped its violent movement, and then the ugly head fell to the ground.

Laneea wrenched out the spear and leaned heavily on it, but she looked at Hunter with a triumphant expression on her face. Raaskar touched her arm and nodded. Then he gave Hunter a tired smile.

"Grala," he said. "They hide in these holes. It would have taken your head off with one bite."

"They make good eating," Laneea said, still breathing hard from the sudden exertion. "We will broil some tonight."

"I hope not the head," Hunter grinned crookedly. Looking from Laneea to Raaskar, he added, "You saved my life."

"That we did," Laneea agreed. She pointed at her foot. "You probably saved mine when you invited us into your winter-home. Your Healer-woman made my leg whole again. I owe you a great debt."

"Not anymore."

Raaskar proceeded to pull the headless sinuous body out of the hole. It flopped onto the hard ground. Then he cut off chunks of meat and wrapped them into pieces of leather which he had removed from his backpack.

"How will you broil them?" Hunter asked, curious. "We have no fire or any means to make one."

Smiling mysteriously, Raaskar said, "We will. I am familiar with these tunnels and I know where I can find what we need." He rose. "This has made my body warm." With those words, he stripped off his fur. Laneea and Raas-ini followed his example. Now they only wore thin shirts and short kilts fashioned from soft leather.

Looking at the two women, Hunter found them particularly attractive, especially Raas-ini. A couple of warrior women with their spears.

The Jnaar rolled their furs into bundles and tied them with leather straps. Raaskar turned to Hunter, "It should be safe now to put your suits into that opening."

Hunter approached the hole, still apprehensive and cautious, gingerly stepping over the lifeless body of the Grala. Before he shoved his suit into the small cave, he threw a quick look at Raaskar.

"You're sure it's safe?"

The Jnaar nodded and smiled. "Quite safe."

Pushing the suit through the large opening, Hunter murmured, "I hope it'll still be in one piece when we come back." Stepping away from the hole, he signaled Cameron and Malone. "Apparently, it's okay now."

The two men added their suits to Hunter's. It seemed Cameron felt the same way Hunter did. "What if another of those monstrosities decides to move in?"

Hunter shrugged. "Maybe we'll have a heat wave by then and we won't need them."

"That'll mean it is summer outside," Malone commented. "I hope we'll be on our way home before that."

"Well, so do I, but I'm prepared to stay until we either find Regina or know what happened to her," Hunter said, not hiding his irritation.

"That's fine by me," Malone growled. "This is probably better and more exciting than sitting around inside that oval prison day in and day out, twiddling our thumbs and looking at the damned screen all day long."

Hunter glanced at Cameron, waiting for his comment, but the bearded man stayed silent. "I guess we're ready to move on," Hunter said. "From now on we'd better be on guard. It seems these tunnels are not exactly safe. Keep you weapons ready."

The three Jnaar were already on the move and the humans walked briskly to catch up with them. Hunter moved his head slowly back and forth, letting the beam of his headlamp play across the ground and the walls, sometimes even the ceiling. One never knew what could be hiding glued against the damp surface above their heads.

They came upon a spot where another tunnel joined theirs. Raaskar took the new tunnel. The new one split after they traveled for a couple of hours. It split again soon after. They went into the wider one.

"One can easily get lost in here," Malone remarked. "We're lucky we have a guide."

"Without the Jnaar, we would have never entered these tunnels," Hunter said.

"How will we find our way back?" Even though Malone spoke calmly, Hunter detected concern in the big man's voice.

"That won't be a problem. Dawn will guide us back."

"Who's Dawn?"

Hunter lifted his left arm so Malone could see the gadget on his wrist. "This is Dawn."

"Your wrist-computer. You call it Dawn? Sounds like a girl's name. Why?"

"An ex-girlfriend," Hunter said curtly, tired of explaining to everybody who asked why he called a computer Dawn. "You have a problem with that?"

"Not me." Malone glanced at Cameron, who walked beside him. "What do you call yours?"

"It doesn't have a name. Mine isn't like Hunter's."

"I had a sidearm once I called Red Heat," Malone mused. "Couldn't miss a target with that one, but I traded it in for a newer, better model, which didn't work as well for me. And then there was this guy in my outfit who had a knife he named Mister Steel. I won't go into details about the things he did with that knife. He was a sick man. One of his compatriots drilled a hole through his skull one day."

"You can't compare Dawn with a gun or a knife," Hunter said, defensively. "She's not some kind of tool you use and throw away or trade in. She's self-aware."

"An AI. I understand." Malone nodded. "I've heard about those. Never seen one."

"Well, now you have."

Malone snorted. After a short pause, he let out a rumbling laugh. "You're quite sensitive when it comes to that gadget of yours. Looks like you've formed some kind of bond with it. Being alone a lot does that to a guy, especially if you don't have any friends."

Hunter didn't know why Malone's remarks rubbed him the wrong way. "You seem to be an expert in those matters. For your information, I do have friends back at the Station. Wong is one of them."

"If he's such a good friend, why isn't he here with us?"

"He was going to come, but Professor Tennenboum needed him to look after the main computer. He's the only one who knows how to repair it should something go wrong. To be honest, I wish he were here."

"Instead of me?" Malone sounded disappointed.

"I won't deny it. Yes, instead of you." Hunter shrugged, not wanting to antagonize the big man more than he already had. "Perhaps it's because I don't know you well enough. It takes time to develop a friendship."

"I've never had many close friends," Malone said. "A mercenary can't afford to get close to someone. People die too quickly in my profession."

"Why did you become a mercenary?"

"Bad luck, I suppose. I never knew my father or mother. My mother was a whore who left me in an orphanage after I was born. I grew up fighting for survival in a poor neighborhood in Old-Lond. My body is covered with badly healed scars inflicted by knives and other weapons. When I was old enough, I joined the military. After a few years of that, I got tired of the constant drill and discipline, so I left. I didn't have a profession, but I was good at warfare, so I began hiring out my services."

Hunter didn't comment. It seemed Malone had been dealt a bad hand by fate. It wasn't his fault if he came across as somewhat coarse and uneducated.

He didn't know if it was his imagination, but somehow it seemed brighter in the tunnel, and then the tunnel ended in a large cave. He blinked against the sudden light and suppressed an exclamation of surprise when he saw the vegetation. Small shrubs dotted the ground. There were even a few short trees with feathery branches.

Raaskar gave him a happy grin. "We will stop here and rest. This is where we will find sticks to make a fire. By the way, you don't need your light in here."

Hunter stared at the ceiling. It was covered with dots of bright lights. "What are those things?"

"Fire-rocks," Raaskar explained. "I told you it would get brighter."

"Can you analyze those?" Hunter addressed Dawn, keeping his voice low.

"From what I can detect at this distance, those are radioactive crystals." She spoke silently in his mind.

"Are they a danger to humans?"

"No. In fact they are probably quite beneficial. I will try to examine them in more detail."

"This is unbelievable," Malone exclaimed, walking deeper into the cave. "Like an underground world. Is that a small pond over there?" He looked at Raaskar, but then he seemed to realize the Jnaar couldn't understand him. His gaze switched to Hunter. "I believe I see water."

Hunter saw it also. "Is that water clean?" he asked Raaskar.

The alien man nodded. "We can drink from it," he said.

When Malone started to head for the pond, Raaskar spoke sharply. "Don't move!"

Even though Malone didn't understand him, he stopped in mid-stride. "What?"

All three aliens stood motionless. Their large, purple eyes perused the cave and they appeared to listen intently. They all relaxed at the same time. Laneea and Raas-ini began walking toward the pond.

Raaskar gave Hunter a quick nod. "It is safe. You can proceed."

"Did you expect trouble?" Hunter asked.

"I always do," Raaskar acknowledged. "Anything can hide among these plants. Even when it seems safe, you must never let down your guard. We share these tunnels and caverns with many life forms. Not all are friendly."

"I'll remember that. Thanks for the warning. I'm glad you're with us."

Raaskar's smile showed his appreciation. "Your people gave us shelter and saved Laneea from spending the rest of her life as a cripple. To keep you safe is a small price to pay."

The females reached the pond before the men did. Laughing happily, Raas-ini dipped her foot into the water. "It is cool and refreshing." Then she began stripping off her clothes. Laneea did the same. Hunter, of course, had seen Raas-ini without clothes before and knew what she looked like naked. Looking at Laneea's body, he had to admit she was as trim and lovely as her daughter.

It was hard to believe she was eighty years old.

When Malone and Cameron stepped around the shrubs, the women were already wading into the pool, chattering happily.

"They're naked," Malone observed, stating the obvious and staring at them.

Beside Hunter, Raaskar also took off his clothes. Then he joined his mate and daughter, cutting the water with powerful strokes.

"You look as if you've never seen a naked woman before," Hunter said to Malone.

Malone chuckled good-humoredly. "I have, but it's been awhile. None as lovely as these two, though."

"I have," Cameron said with a thoughtful expression on his face. "The daughters of the Xandra have perfect bodies like these two."

"Your fiancée has a nice body," Malone said.

When Cameron turned to look at him, Malone added hastily, "Don't take this the wrong way, Cameron. I'm just saying she is also beautiful."

"That she is," Cameron agreed. "In fact, most of the women on Nu-Eden had great bodies after the Xandra recreated them."

"Are you saying your fiancée has been recreated?"

"No. She's still a real human. If she weren't, she would have stayed on Nu-Eden."

Hunter noticed the pond wasn't deep. He had been watching Raas-ini swimming back and forth. Now she rose and stood submerged up to her waist in the water, her lovely breasts exposed to anyone's view. She threw a glance in his direction and turned to face him. Smiling coyly, she raised her arms behind her head and squeezed the water out of her hair. The movement lifted her breasts to make her nipples point upwards. Memories of suckling those thick nipples only the night before made his loins flutter gently. Damn it. He'd better control himself.

Raaskar swam back toward shore. "You should take advantage of this water to cleanse your bodies," he suggested. "We won't get another opportunity for a while."

"You're right," Hunter agreed. Turning to his companions, he explained. "Raaskar says it'll be some time until we get another chance to wash ourselves. I'm going to jump in." With that he began taking off his shirt.

Malone and Cameron shrugged and followed his example. With his clothes on, Malone appeared robust and large, but naked he looked even more massive. His body was heavily muscled, solid, with a thick neck and corded thighs. Hunter noticed the scars on his body. Even the tattoos couldn't hide them. Cameron was slim with a good body, his muscles defined like those of an athlete.

Sliding into the water, Hunter enjoyed the cool liquid on his skin. He scrubbed his body with his hands, trying to wash off the perspiration, wishing he had a bar of soap to really clean himself.

"The last time I enjoyed a dip in an outdoor pool was on Nu-Eden," Cameron said. His eyes searched the shrubs surrounding the pond as if expecting something to appear. "This looks so peaceful, but is it?"

"Raaskar said it was safe," Hunter assured him.

"Do you trust him?"

"I do. I believe he and I have become friends."

Cameron smirked. "You mean that young filly and you have become good friends."

Hunter gave him a sharp look. "What do you know?"

"I saw you two going into one of the storage rooms a few days ago. I didn't have to guess what you were doing."

Hunter searched out Malone, who sat nearby submerged in the water, only his head sticking above the surface, his eyes closed. "Does he know?"

Cameron shook his head. "Don't worry. I'm not the kind of guy who blabs to everybody. Your love life is none of my business. Your secret is safe. Do her parents know about you two?"

Looking in the direction of the Jnaar, Hunter shrugged. "Her mother might. I'm not sure."

"Perhaps they know but don't care. They are aliens with a different morality. The whole universe doesn't follow the rules and morals of the human race." Cameron rubbed his bearded face. "We should have packed some soap."

"Funny, I was thinking the same thing before." Hunter let out a surprised grunt when something touched his leg. Then he felt fingers circling his penis, but only for a moment. Before he could react, a body burst out of the water in front of him and slithered up his front. Soft breasts teased his chest.

Raas-ini laughed as she pushed away from him, floating on her back, her breasts and pussy clearly visible for a quick moment before she twisted her body and dove back under the surface.

Cameron let out a little snicker. "If they didn't know before they do now, Hunter. Your secret's out."

Hunter cursed under his breath. The last thing he needed was create bad blood between him and the Jnaar, but when he looked at Raaskar, he didn't give any indication he had even noticed his daughter's little play. Perhaps he didn't, and if he did, he might not care. Like Cameron said, they had different morals.

Malone rose out of the water. "I'm going out," he announced. "Taking long baths is not one of my favorite pastimes. Since I can't swim, I've never had the desire to go swimming. Besides, I don't want my body to get waterlogged." He waded toward shore.

"I've also had enough," Cameron said, following the big man.

As if on cue, the three aliens also climbed back on shore. Hunter wasn't quite ready yet to leave this little bit of heaven. It had been months since he enjoyed a swim in the lake by the Station, before the water became too cold. He didn't know when he would have the pleasure again. Floating on his back, he watched the two women, especially enjoying the view of their deliciously round buttocks.

Sighing, he closed his eyes for a moment, wondering what lay ahead. He didn't know how to handle the situation with Raas-ini. He was captivated by her beauty and by her gentle and yet fierce nature. There was something about her he found exciting, something that went beyond the exhilarating feeling a new relationship creates. Being with her made him happy and he wished he could experience this feeling for the rest of his life. Could it be that he was in love with this alien girl?

Deep down he knew their relationship could not work. They were from two different species, probably could never have children because of their different ways of reproduction. The Jnaar laid eggs. Humans bore live young. Jnaar lived for four hundred years, while humans were lucky to reach a hundred and fifty.

Yet he longed for Raas-ini's passionate embrace, longed to hear her ecstatic moans while he moved between her strong but soft thighs, suckling on her young breasts…

He stopped his thoughts when he felt a stirring in his penis. It wouldn't do to climb back on land with an erection.

Submerging his lower body briefly under water he waited until he was sure everything was relaxed before he waded back to shore. The others were already getting dressed. He rubbed his body with his hands to dry himself, not wanting to put his clothes over his wet skin. The air in the cavern seemed surprisingly dry and he was aware of a slight breeze. It didn't take long before he felt dry enough to get dressed.

"I will gather dry branches for a fire," Raaskar announced. "We will eat fresh meat."

"Won't it take too long to broil meat?" Hunter asked.

"We have enough time. We will sleep here and get some rest. Tomorrow will be a long day because the next resting place is not close. We don't want to sleep in the tunnels. It is not safe."

Hunter didn't question Raaskar's decision. He trusted the Jnaar, with his life if necessary. When he told Malone and Cameron about the plan to make this cavern their first stop, they didn't argue.

"This is better than I ever hoped," Malone said. "Who would have thought we'd find a place like this underground?"

Chapter Eleven

The sizzling chunks of meat from the giant snake created a mouthwatering aroma, and when Raaskar offered pieces to the humans they accepted them. None of them were finicky when it came to eating meat from unknown animals, as long as the meat was not raw.

Even though the meat was a bit charcoaled in places and had a peculiar flavor, Hunter nevertheless enjoyed it. "I've eaten meat from wild game much greasier than this," he said as he licked off his fingers. "There is nothing better than eating fresh meat broiled over an open flame after a hunt. Makes me almost homesick."

Cameron grinned. "I wouldn't exactly say this is meat from some game we've hunted."

"But it was prepared over a real fire," Hunter reiterated. He looked at Malone. "When was the last time you ate something not cooked over an artificial heat source?"

The big man tore his gaze away from the flickering flames at which he'd been staring, letting his eyes focus on Hunter. He seemed to have been lost in some long forgotten memories. "I'm sorry, what was that you said?"

"I wondered when you ate something like this last."

"It seems an eternity ago since I sat around a campfire," Malone said. "It feels so peaceful here."

"It does, doesn't it?" Hunter agreed. "Yet I bet it isn't as peaceful as it appears. I've been watching the Jnaar. They look relaxed, but only because they're in a familiar environment. Their senses are alert to dangers we can't even imagine. We can't let this serene atmosphere lull us into a false feeling of security."

Hunter wiped his hands on a large leaf and threw it into the fire. It flared up briefly, curling up to be consumed by the hot flames.

"Nu-Eden was this peaceful," Cameron said, thoughtfully. "The danger lurked unseen and unnoticed everywhere. It was too late when we realized Paradise had a snake hiding in the grass."

Malone chuckled. "The snake we're eating was hiding in a deep hole, not in the grass. It almost took off Hunter's head. I hope there aren't too many of these creatures lying in ambush waiting for unwary travelers like us."

Raaskar had been listening to their conversation. "What are your friends saying?" he asked Hunter.

"They're wondering if we can expect to be attacked by other Grala."

Raaskar smiled grimly. "The Grala are not the greatest danger found in these tunnels. The worst of them all are the Dal Losos. They are not easy to kill because they are already dead."

"I've met and fought them," Hunter said, remembering his first encounter with those monstrosities. Visions of emaciated creatures with expressionless faces, hollow cheeks, and dead eyes rose in his mind. He could almost hear the Sras girl, Arlee, as she sobbed. "They are Maklos, children of unions between Sras males and the Siiris."

He hadn't known what she meant at the time, not until later. "The Sras call them Maklos and Makrees," he said. "Dead Faces and Dead Eyes."

"You've met the Sras?" Raaskar said.

Hunter nodded. "We saved a family of them from Keeras. We became friends."

More than friends. Professor Tennenboum had sex with one of their women and Hunter sampled the sweet body of Arlee. He glanced at Raas-ini with a sudden flash of guilt. He had been more than attracted to the young Sras girl. Given more time with her, he may even have developed the same feelings he had for Raas-ini.

"The Jnaar and the Sras are not friends," Raaskar said.

"So I've been told." Hunter remembered Professor Tennenboum talking about it. "Tell me why?"

"I cannot give you a reason." Raaskar used his new knife to cut off another piece of greasy meat. "Our races have been feuding as long as anyone can remember."

"So what will happen if we run into them?"

Raaskar shrugged. "We will fight."

"Not if I can help it," Hunter said.

"How will you stop it?"

"By talking to them."

Raaskar gave him a questioning look. "They will not understand."

"Of course they will. I speak their language." Hunter smiled, enjoying Raaskar's surprise.

The Jnaar studied Hunter with a thoughtful expression. "You have surely been blessed by the gods, Hunter. They've given you many gifts. The ability to communicate with a stranger who doesn't speak your tongue is one of them."

Hunter indicated his wrist. "I learn with the help of this."

"I've observed you talking to it," Raaskar said. "Does it talk back to you?"

"It does." Hunter pointed at his head. "It speaks to me inside my head. Only I can hear it." That was not the truth, but he didn't see any reason to reveal all the things Dawn could do.

"The Elders tell us our race once had devices like that. On the world we came from. Now we are like the Sras, primitive and savage. We have forgotten everything our ancestors knew."

"In time, your children will discover new things. Perhaps someday you will travel to the stars again and go back to the world from which your people came."

Hunter didn't quite believe it. How could a race of people living below ground for much of the time even develop aspirations to visit the stars hidden above the clouds? He wondered if the descendants of the humans stranded on this planet would fall back into savagery should they be forgotten by Earth.

"My people struggle just to survive and the only desire we have is to have a full belly and live in peace. The young who venture outside these caves do not wonder what those lights in the night sky are. If those are unknown worlds like the Elders tell us, we have no desire to travel to those worlds. Who's to say those worlds are better than this one? If they were so wonderful why did our ancestors leave them?"

"They probably left because your home worlds became overcrowded like ours did. Or perhaps they just wanted to see what lay beyond. Your people are probably very much like ours. We're curious. We need to know what's out there. We're all looking for that better world, for Paradise."

Raaskar spit a piece of gristle into the fire, making it flare up for a moment. He wiped his mouth with the back of his hand.

"Our legends speak of such a place beyond the mountains," he said, staring into the flames. "It is a beautiful valley with little snow in the winter. There are few clouds in the sky and it is always warm. Herds of Thrall are plentiful and the lake is filled with creatures whose flesh tastes sweet and clean." His gaze fastened on Hunter. "You see, we do not need to travel to distant worlds. All we have to do is cross those mountains."

"So why don't you?"

The Jnaar chuckled softly. "There is no way to cross them. Most of the ones who tried perished. Their bleached skeletons were found by hunters and other brave adventurers who were lucky to return. That beautiful valley is still only a legend."

"There will always be those," Hunter said. He yawned, suddenly feeling tired. "Those fire-rocks in the ceiling, do they ever get dim?"

"No." Raaskar shook his head.

"Then how can you keep track of the passing of time?"

"The Timekeepers are responsible for that, but if you are asking how we know when to sleep, it is not difficult. We just follow the cycle of the sirril plants."

"You rely on a plant to tell you when to sleep and when to rise?"

"Not entirely. Our bodies tell us. In fact, my body tells me it is almost time to sleep now." He smiled. "Your body is telling you the same thing."

Hunter yawned again. "I guess we just lie down and close our eyes. I'm used to having it dark when I go to sleep."

"So are we. In our village, we have houses with dark rooms for sleeping, but here we have no choice but to sleep with the light. You get used to it."

Hunter turned to Malone and Cameron. "We'll stay here for the night."

"Night?" Cameron looked at the bright ceiling.

"Just a figure of speech. Those lights never go dim." He rose from his sitting position. "I'm going to the pond to wash my hands. This snake meat was greasy."

Malone wiped his hands on the carpet of grass-like vegetation. "This is good enough for me," he said. He looked around. "I suggest we stay together. Perhaps we should take turns watching, just in case we get unwelcome visitors."

"I'll set up a safe perimeter around our camp," Cameron said, touching his wrist. "This is actually a Guard-Dog, just one of its functions. It will alert me if anything large approaches."

"So will my gadget," Hunter said, "but by then it may already be too late. I'll ask Raaskar what he intends to do." Hunter looked at the alien. "Is one of us staying awake to watch?"

"Yes. My daughter will take the first watch," the Jnaar said.

"All right. I can take the next if you want."

Raaskar nodded, and Hunter turned to walk to the pond. The vegetation felt soft under his boots and when he reached the pond, he looked across the water. Seeing a few small leafy plants floating on its surface, he thought of the stories Cameron told him about Nu-Eden and the mysterious alien woman on a plant. Squatting down, he dipped his hands into the water and rubbed them together, washing away the grease. Wiping his face with wet hands, he ran his fingers through his hair in an effort to dry his hands.

When he came back to his companions, they had already bedded down. He searched for a good spot and lay down, using his backpack for a pillow, but not before looking at Raas-ini, who sat cross-legged in front of the small fire.

She saw him looking and gave him a small smile. "You will be safe," she said with a low voice.

He noticed the spear beside her and hoped she knew how to use it as effectively as her parents, should it become necessary. Closing his eyes, he tried to relax and sleep, but his thoughts kept him awake. He had come close to death or at least being seriously injured. Only Raaskar's quick reaction and knowledge of the dangers had saved him. Not for the first time he was happy to have the aliens with them. He wondered why Dawn had not alerted him.

"Because those crystals in the rocks are interfering with my detection-system," she said silently, aware of his thoughts. "I'm afraid I won't be much help to you when it comes to warning you of approaching dangers."

"It'll take me awhile to get used to that," he answered. "I've come to depend on you perhaps a little too much."

"Sorry," she said. "Now sleep."

* * * *

Aware of someone shaking his shoulder gently, Hunter opened his eyes to see Raas-ini bending over him. "It is your turn," she whispered.

He rubbed his eyes. "But I haven't even slept yet," he complained.

She smiled. "You have. I thought you'd never wake."

When he looked at the illuminated crystal on his gadget, he realized he had slept for nearly three hours. Sitting up, he looked at his companions. All of them were fast asleep.

"Come," Raas-ini said, taking his hand and pulling him up.

His look questioned her. "Where are we going?"

She smiled wickedly and whispered, "Don't ask questions. Let me show you."

She pulled him with her toward a clump of shrubs and led him to the other side. Then she removed her shirt and slipped out of her short kilt. She stood naked in front of him.

"What are you waiting for? Take off your clothes." When she saw his perplexed expression, she laughed quietly and came close. "You are lucky I let you sleep this long, but now I need to feel you inside me." She tugged on his pants. "We don't have much time. Don't waste it asking questions."

Against his better judgment, he undressed and took her into his arms. Her skin felt warm and her breasts lay soft against his chest. Kissing her fiercely, he pushed her onto the ground. She lay down and opened her thighs. Rolling between them, he probed for the entrance to her love-channel and found her wet and ready. Sliding his stiff mast into her slippery sheath, he pushed deep. She heaved up against him, letting out a stifled cry as she took him into her.

She folded her legs around his thighs and writhed beneath him with violent movements, her arms wrapped around his back for support. He pounded between her clutching thighs for a long time, shutting out the world around him. For a while he was happy and carefree, not aware of anything else but the ecstatic moans of the girl beneath him and the joy he found in her arms.

When his final moment came, he dug his fingers into her buttocks and held her, filling her with his gift, trying to suppress his grunts of pleasure. She experienced her orgasm at the same time as he did and her soft cries seemed loud in his ears as she milked him fiercely.

Spent and satisfied, he relaxed into her arms and lay on top of her soft body, gasping for air.

"You gave me much pleasure," she panted, squeezing his semi-erect penis with her strong inner muscles. "I am glad you are here with me. I would have hated to leave you."

He kissed her gently. "I am also glad I'm here. Do your parents know about us?"

"I told my mother."

"How about your father?"

She gave a small giggle. "He probably knows."

"They have no objections? I mean to you and I, our people are so different from each other. How can that ever work?"

"They don't care. Why should they?" Her sex-organ throbbed around his penis, making him groan. She giggled again. "We may be different in many ways, but there is no problem with this. We fit together quite nicely."

"Maybe too nicely," he said, his breath catching in his throat as a surge of pleasure pulsed through him. "I've become addicted to you and I don't know how to stop it."

"Why would you want to stop it? You make me feel good and I know I bring you joy. There is no reason for us to ever part again." Her purple eyes searched his face. "I am in love with you, Hunter."

"Are you sure you're in love with me or just the pleasure I give you?"

"Of course I love the pleasure you give me, but I love you. You are strong and forceful, a brave warrior, but you are also kind and gentle. I will gladly be your mate if you want me."

A little shocked by her forwardness, he gave her a lopsided grin. "If that was a marriage proposal then you are a bold young woman. Where I grew up it was the male who asked the female if she wanted to become his bride."

"That makes no sense. My people have no such rules. If a female wants a male, she tells him so. I'm telling you I want you." She gave his penis another squeeze and then she pushed against his chest. "It is time for me to sleep. I am tired now."

He pulled out of her and knelt between her spread thighs. "I thought you wanted to play some more."

"I did before, but now I am not in the mood anymore." She slid away from him and closed her thighs. Rising, she picked up her clothes and donned them.

He watched her silently. Then he stood up and stepped in front of her. "What's wrong? Did I say something to offend you?"

Her face was without expression. "It is not the words you said. It is what you didn't say."

"Which is what?"

"It doesn't matter. You are right. There is a great difference between your people and mine. It would never work." With that she stepped around him and walked back toward the small camp.

He looked after her, shaking his head, puzzled by her behavior. This was a side of her he hadn't seen before. He knew she had fire but she also had a temper. This little wildcat needed taming.

Grinning, he got dressed. Then he followed her slowly. Everyone appeared to be asleep. Raas-ini lay beside her mother, her eyes closed. He didn't think she was already sleeping, but he didn't say anything and just sat down. The fire had died, not even embers were glowing. However, there was no need for a fire. The temperature in the cavern was warm and pleasant.

Sitting on his haunches, his laser rifle resting in his lap, he studied Raas-ini's sleeping face. She was so beautiful. Now he found her more desirable than ever.

It seemed to be brighter than before, but he knew it was an illusion. His eyes had adjusted to the level of brightness in the cavern. He wondered how it would be to live with this constant light all the time, never finding a change. Of course, anyone seeking darkness could just wander into the tunnels. He also wondered if the light-emitting crystals were in every cavern across the planet or if they were just an anomaly in this part of Iceworld.

"How long have I been sitting here?" he asked Dawn.

"About two hours. You should get some more sleep. You are still tired," Dawn answered.

"I don't feel tired."

"You may not feel tired, but I detect a level of exhaustion that can only be remedied by another couple of hours sleep. It is never a good idea to exert your body by having sex when you're on a mission. Go wake up Raaskar." Her silent voice sounded like a command in his mind.

He had made it a habit of listening to Dawn's advice. She never steered him wrong. Walking over to Raaskar, he touched the Jnaar on the shoulder. Like an alert animal, Raaskar's eyes flew open, his hand shot up to grab Hunter by the throat, but then he seemed to realize where he was and relaxed his grip.

"Your turn to keep watch," Hunter said with a low voice, not wanting to wake up the others. He rubbed his throat.

Raaskar nodded and rose. Clapping Hunter on the shoulder, he moved to the spot Hunter had vacated. Lowering his body onto his folded legs, he again nodded to Hunter but remained silent.

Hunter went back to his earlier sleeping spot and lay down. He didn't know if he could fall asleep, but the last thing he remembered was Dawn's silent voice, "Sleep."

Chapter Twelve

They traveled for four days through the dark tunnels, sleeping inside a tiny cave two nights in a row and in a small cavern illuminated by fire-rocks the next. Raas-ini did not offer to have sex with Hunter, and he wondered why. When he tried to talk to her, she gave him short answers. Not wanting to draw any attention to his intimate relationship with her, he left it alone. The trek through the tunnels was strenuous and he heeded Dawn's warning not to exert himself by spending part of his resting period having sex with the Jnaar girl.

"I can soothe your yearning for release of your sexual tension by manipulating your pleasure centers without you having to waste any precious energy," she suggested, but he declined her offer.

"It's not the same, Dawn. I need to feel Raas-ini's naked warm skin on mine."

"I can give you the illusion of that," Dawn said, sounding like a seductress. He knew she could do that, but he turned her down. "I want the real thing."

Dawn didn't take offense. "I understand. I'll be here if you change your mind."

He chuckled softly, wondering if it was her idea of a joke. "You are always here."

On the fourth day, their presence was challenged by a group of Monkeys. The moment the small party of travelers stepped into the cavern, they were greeted with the high-pitched shrill cries of the four-armed humanoid creatures. Hunter had seen the elusive humanoids only a couple of times on his trips into the neighboring forest near the Station, but he had never seen so many in one group. He estimated around four or five dozen were milling around the only pool.

Many of them were females with young ones clinging to their hairy bodies. The males gathered in front of the females, forming a protective wall, waving their four long and bony arms threateningly. They bellowed with loud cries, warning the humans not to come any closer.

Raaskar stopped walking and lifted a hand. "They won't attack us, but we can't stay here," he said. "We must travel around them. There are too many to fight."

"They're no match against our weapons," Hunter said.

"I know, but we cannot kill them without a good reason. Killing a Wiook may anger the gods. There really are no good reasons to kill Wiooks. They are peaceful and not aggressive, but they will fight us if we insist on staying here. Their sharp claws can inflict serious injuries."

"I was looking forward to a bath." Hunter looked with longing at the calm water of the pond, feeling grubby from days of traveling in the dusty tunnels.

"There is another but smaller cavern with a pond not far. We'll have to go there to clean up and rest," Raaskar told them. "Just walk slowly. Don't make any aggressive moves and we won't have any problems." He was the first one to head for the wall to the right of the pond, walking with slow, measured steps. Laneea and Raas-ini stayed close to him, their eyes on the Wiooks. Hunter noticed their white knuckles as they gripped their spears.

"What's happening?" Malone asked.

"We'll try to get past them," Hunter explained. "They won't attack unless we give them a reason. We're heading for the next cavern." He followed the three Jnaar slowly, watching the four-armed creatures with misgivings.

When they reached the end of the cavern, they found two tunnels. Raaskar chose the one on the left.

"Where does the other tunnel lead?" Hunter asked.

"A beautiful cavern, but it is populated by Sras," Raaskar said. "We would not be welcome there."

"How long still until we come to your winter city?"

"We will sleep twice, and then we should be there."

"I'm looking forward to meeting your people and to see how you survive the long winter," Hunter said.

The next two days passed without any memorable events, except for another giant snake that tried to sneak up on them while they slept. Cameron was the one who spotted it after his Guard-Dog alerted him to the reptile's presence. He dispatched it with his laser. It provided them with another feast of broiled meat.

After resting for a few hours, they traveled for most of the next day. Then they arrived at the winter city of Raaskar's people.

The cavern they entered was enormous. Hunter spotted huge, thick pillars rising from the floor to support a ceiling much higher than the ones in the other caverns they had encountered until now. This cavern seemed to stretch for many kilometers.

"Welcome to my world," Raas-ini said, making a circular motion with her arm. Her smile spoke of the joy she felt to be home again. It was also the first friendly smile she gave Hunter since their last lovemaking.

"It is beautiful," Hunter said. He looked at Raaskar. "You told me of a beautiful valley beyond the mountains. This, to me, looks like such a place."

"It seems beautiful and it is, but it is not a peaceful place. We have to be on guard against raids from the Shadow-dwellers and attacks by the Sras and the Dal Losos. Dangerous animals roam the tunnels and the caverns. No, my friend, this is not the valley of our legends."

As they moved deeper into the cavern, a group of young Jnaar warriors, armed with spears and bows suddenly confronted them. Raaskar stepped in front of the humans, slapped his right fist against his left shoulder.

"I am Raaskar, son of Aarkas. I have returned from the hunt in the painted mountains."

The leader of the group tried to look past Raaskar. "I recognize you, Raaskar, son of Aarkas. I am Ruukas. Before you are allowed to proceed you must answer my questions. Nobody hunts at the time of palos. Where are the furs of the animals you hunted? Where is the meat? Who are the strangers with you?"

"Many questions," Raaskar said. "My mate was injured and our hunting party left us behind. I had no means to transport any meat or furs. We were lucky to survive."

"Who are the strangers?" the young warrior asked again.

"These strangers are visitors from another world. They saved us and offered us their hospitality. They are my friends."

"Why did you bring them here?"

"They are looking for one of their females. She was captured by our people and they are hoping to find her here."

Ruukas shook his head. His purple eyes studied Hunter, who had moved to Raaskar's side.

"She is not here. We've never seen people like these before. The male beside you has black skin. He is different from the other two, of which one has his face covered with hair."

"They may not look the same, but they are of the same species." Raaskar looked at Hunter and smiled. "You can introduce yourself."

Hunter touched his left shoulder with his right fist. "I am Hunter. It's an honor to meet you, Ruukas. My companions and I offer you peace and the friendship of our people."

The young Jnaar warrior gave him an astonished look. "You speak our language?"

"I do," Hunter acknowledged.

"You carry no spears or bows?"

Hunter smiled and lifted his laser rifle. "This is my weapon. It throws bolts of lightning. I have killed Keeras and the majestic Krill with it."

"Does he speak the truth?" Ruukas looked at Raaskar.

Raaskar nodded solemnly. "He speaks the truth. The strangers have magical weapons, like the weapons our ancestors possessed. It is good to have them as friends."

Ruukas smiled thinly. "If those weapons really do what you say, I don't want the strangers as enemies. There is one more test I must perform." His gaze lay on Raas-ini and Laneea.

Laneea moved forward and bared her breast. Ruukas bent and took her nipple into his mouth. A moment later, he straightened, smiled and turned to speak to his companions. "They have passed the test. Let them through." He stepped aside and made room on the narrow path. "Welcome back home, Raaskar."

"It is good to be home," Raaskar said.

"What was that all about?" Hunter asked Raaskar.

"What?"

"Why did he suck on Laneea's breast?"

"To confirm we are who we say we are."

"I don't understand."

"You would if you'd ever tasted the breast of a female Shadow-dweller."

"I hope you're not talking about those ugly monstrosities you call Dal Losos?" Hunter shook himself, visions of emaciated female bodies appearing in his mind's eye. "Who'd want to suck on those flaps of skin?"

Raaskar chuckled, amused by Hunter's display of disgust. "Not the Dal Losos as you've seen them, but as they were before they changed. Most of the females were beautiful and alluring and the males handsome."

Before Hunter could ask more questions, another group of Jnaar appeared. Two males and two females, all of them older than the group of warriors they had encountered. They were accompanied by three small cat-like animals.

One of the males stopped. "Raaskar. You have finally returned. We did not expect you to survive."

Raaskar laughed and slapped his hand against the other male's shoulder. "As you can see we are alive. The gods have favored us." Turning, he pointed at the three humans. "These strangers are my friends. They helped us and now they came to ask for our help."

The Jnaar scrutinized Hunter and the others. "They are neither Jnaar nor Sras. What are they?"

"They call themselves humans. They came here from one of the outside worlds far away, like our ancestors did. Apparently, they are also stranded on Iceworld." Raaskar looked at Hunter. "This is my older brother Raas."

In the meantime, Laneea and Raas-ini had run to the two females and were hugging them fiercely, emitting little cries of joy.

"They are just like our women," Malone remarked behind Hunter. "It seems we have a lot in common with these people."

Hunter gave Raas the Jnaar greeting. "Peace, brother of Raaskar. I am Hunter."

Raas acted as surprised as Ruukas. He touched his shoulder with his fist. "Peace, Hunter. Where did you learn to speak our language?"

"I've met a tribe of your people before the time of palos at the place where your ancestors lived when they came to Iceworld. I've hunted and shared broiled Thrall with them."

He bent down to stroke the head of the small animal that had come close to sniff his legs. He knew they were called Sreel. The Jnaar used them for tracking.

"Hunter is my friend," Raaskar said.

"If you are my brother's friend then you are also my friend. Welcome to our city." Raas made a little bow and turned to Raaskar. "We will have a celebration in your honor, my brother." He grinned. "You look well for a dead man."

"I may look well, but I am tired from the long journey. We all are. How is my dwelling?"

"It is still waiting for your return."

"And my two sons?"

"They have grown taller in your absence. Rasar is nearly a man."

Raaskar laughed. "So he believes. It is time I came home to put some restraints on him." He clapped Raas on the shoulder. "We will speak more after we have rested."

"Yes, we will. You must talk about your journey. Our father will be happy to see you." Raas and his companions turned into a side path and disappeared behind the tall shrubs as the road made a turn.

The group walked on down the main road. There were houses on either side of the road, nestled among shrubs and trees. Some had stone fronts, but most of them were built from logs. The roofs were covered with branches and dry reeds. Hunter noticed windows and doors, but there wasn't any glass in the windows. The doors however were solid, also made from logs.

They met more Jnaar on the road—some on foot, some rode Leeas, the stocky, black-coated herbivores Hunter had first seen with the Sras. A few sat on Heeskas, the long-legged birds used only by warriors and hunters. Those riders carried bows or spears. Hunter hoped they were going on a hunt and not into battle with the Sras or some other still unknown enemy.

"How many of your people live in this city?" Hunter said to Raaskar.

"I have never counted them, but probably about 1,000. Most of them are still quite young. The Recordkeepers will know." Raaskar pointed to a large body of water visible through the trees. "The next generation of eggs will hatch in there. The birthing place is heavily guarded against animals and raids from the Sras, and the Shadow-dwellers. To be one of the Egg-Guardians is a great honor."

"How many eggs are in there?"

"The numbers are limited to 100 eggs. We have to be careful not to overpopulate. This cavern will support only so many."

"I can see the need for birth control," Hunter agreed. "Even though this cavern is unbelievably huge. Are there many cities like this?"

"Yes, there are, but I cannot tell you how many. When we want to start another settlement, we must travel far into the mountains to find a suitable cavern. The Jnaar are not the only ones growing in numbers. We have to share this world with the Sras, and there are many."

"Perhaps that is the reason the Jnaar and the Sras are at war with each other?" Hunter ventured.

Raaskar shrugged. "Perhaps."

"I see Heeskas and Leeas. Are there other animals living in these caverns?"

"There is one cavern populated by Thrall. We go there sometimes to hunt, but the Sras also hunt Thrall. We limit the number of Thrall we harvest, as do the Sras. That is the reason we hunt outside when the snow is gone."

Hunter nodded, understanding. "It seems you are in agreement with Sras when it comes to ensuring the survival of both your species."

Before Raaskar could comment, a young Jnaar came up to him. "The Observers want to know who these strangers you brought to our city are."

Raaskar looked toward the small assembly of Jnaar who had gathered in what appeared to be some kind of meeting place. Hunter saw four wizened old men sitting on a raised bench. Hunter knew they must be quite old indeed, since the Jnaar kept their youthful looks until a ripe old age. The rest of the crowd maintained a respectful distance from the four old ones.

The humans had garnered many curious looks from the Jnaar they met traveling along the road, but none had stopped to ask about them. Hunter wondered who these four old males were. The messenger had called them

Observers.

"I must go to talk to the Observers," Raaskar told Hunter. "You wait here. Do not move from here." He began walking toward the throng of Jnaar and the four old ones on the bench.

While they waited, a crowd formed a ring around the travelers. Hunter saw Malone fingering his laser rifle and couldn't blame him. He too felt a bit on edge. After all, these people had never seen humans before. Primitive people were always suspicious of strangers, and these would not be an exception. He shifted his backpack on his back and gripped his own weapon. He didn't expect any trouble, but it was always good to be prepared. He would not go down without a fight.

Raas-ini seemed to notice the tension in his stance. She gave him an encouraging smile and touched his arm. "There is nothing to fear," she said with a low voice. "Once my father explains your presence, we'll be free to do as we please."

Hunter glanced at the Jnaar circling them. "They don't look very friendly," he observed.

"Something must have happened to make them behave this way," Laneea said. She addressed one of the watchers, "Why is everyone so hostile?"

"If you don't know that, you may be the reason," the one she spoke to answered.

"We've been away. What happened?"

"The Shadow-dwellers are hiding among our people," the young man told her.

"How? I don't understand."

"I cannot tell you more."

Raaskar came back, accompanied by six big, muscular guards, carrying long spears. Hunter had to smile. If they only knew what kind of weapons they'd be facing should they decide to attack the three humans, they wouldn't act so confident.

"The Observers want to test us," Raaskar told them.

"I've already been tested," Laneea said, obviously growing annoyed.

"Apparently, the usual tests are not reliable anymore. The Shadow-dwellers are becoming more devious." He looked at Hunter. "Tell your companions we must go with these guards. Tell them also not to resist. I don't want to spill the blood of my people. They are only doing this to protect our city."

Hunter turned to Cameron and Malone. "It seems something has happened here that demands we be tested. It has something to do with the Shadow-dwellers. That's all Raaskar knows. I have no idea what kinds of tests we'll have to undergo."

"I don't have a good feeling about this," Malone growled. "I'm not giving up my laser."

"As long as they don't know these are weapons they won't ask for them," Cameron said. "I'm with you, though. I'm not relinquishing my laser either."

One of the guards spoke. "We'll take your bow and spears." Without waiting for an answer, he reached for Raaskar's bow. Laneea and Raas-ini handed their spears to one of the other guards.

"Hang your lasers across your shoulders," Hunter told Cameron and Malone. "We'll act as if they are part of our baggage."

The guards eyed the humans, obviously searching for weapons. "Where are their spears?" one guard asked.

"They don't have any," Raaskar told them.

"No weapons?" The guard seemed suspicious.

"The humans are a peaceful race," Raaskar said.

"That will be determined by the Observers. Now, go." One guard took the lead; the other five formed a cordon around the prisoners. Hunter had no illusions. He knew they were prisoners.

"We could wipe out half this settlement," Malone grumbled, "and not even work up a sweat."

"They would overcome us eventually," Hunter cautioned. "Let's not do anything hasty. I have no desire to die here because of some misunderstanding. Raaskar promised us protection. He's an honorable man. I trust him."

The crowd of watching Jnaar parted to let the party pass through the corridor they formed. They headed for a large building. It had barred windows and solid doors made from strong trees.

"This looks like a prison," Cameron commented. "Somehow I pictured a different welcoming committee. I hope these people give us a fair trial and find us not guilty for whatever crime we've supposedly committed."

Hunter refrained from talking to Raaskar or the two women. Somehow, he thought it best if their consort didn't know he could understand and speak the Jnaar language.

They passed through the thick doors and entered a small vestibule with another door at the end. Pushing the door open, the guard told them to walk into the room on the other side of the door. The room was poorly lit by oil lamps hanging from the ceiling, but after Hunter's eyes adjusted, he saw a long table to one side. The table was made from thin tree trunks, its top rough and uneven. Behind the table sat three men. They appeared as old as the four Observers outside.

The lead-guard spoke to the prisoners, "Do not speak unless you've been asked a question. Do not try to escape. There is no place to run. Do not attempt to harm the Inquisitors. The penalty will be death. Do you understand?" He glared at Raaskar.

Raaskar nodded. "I understand."

"Then instruct the strangers!"

Raaskar said to Hunter in a low voice, "You heard. Make sure your companions follow these orders."

Hunter translated what the guard had said. Malone chuckled grimly. "He'll be the first one I kill," he said with a threatening look at the guard.

It is a good thing the guard didn't understand him, but Hunter shared the big man's attitude. He'd always hated arrogant bullies and this guy certainly fit the image.

The Jnaar did not miss Malone's hostile look. He gave Malone a hard stare, and then he moved against one wall to join the other guards, his watchful eyes on the prisoners.

One of the old men behind the table looked at Raaskar and made a motion with one hand. "Step forward."

Raaskar followed the order. He stood waiting silently in front of the three Inquisitors.

"What are you called?"

"Raaskar, son of Aarkas."

"I am told you were absent for a long time. Where have you been?"

"I was left behind by my hunting party when my mate injured herself. She could not walk."

"She walks now."

"She was healed by the humans."

"The humans." The old Jnaar's eyes moved to look at Hunter who stood beside Raas-ini. "I suppose he is one of them. Who are these humans?"

"They are travelers from another world."

"And where do they live?"

"In a giant egg that rests on top of the snow."

"You've seen this giant egg?"

"Yes. My mate Laneea, my daughter Raas-ini, and I lived inside the egg until Laneea's leg was fully healed. The humans have magical machines that restore injured parts of a body."

"The Dark Goddess can restore injured parts," one of the other Inquisitors said. "Perhaps these so-called humans are Shadow-dwellers."

"The humans are not Shadow-dwellers," Raaskar said patiently. "They do not worship the Dark Goddess. They have never heard of the Dark Goddess or the Shadow-dwellers."

Hunter knew that was not quite the truth. The Jnaar he'd met by the ruins of the old settlement told him about the Shadow-dwellers. Raaskar was smart not to mention that.

"Why did you bring these three humans to our city?" the first one inquired.

"One of their females was abducted by Jnaar. They hoped to find her here. I've been asked these questions before when we came out of the tunnel."

"I did not ask you for that information. Answer only what I ask you!" the Inquisitor raised his voice slightly. "We haven't heard of a strange female brought here."

Raaskar stood without saying anything, his face without emotion.

The third Inquisitor, who had been silently listening, spoke. "Don't you want to know why you are here in our presence?"

"Of course I want to know. I was told not to speak until asked," Raaskar said.

"Yes, that." The old Jnaar waved his hand in a dismissing gesture. "You may speak freely."

"Why are we here?" Raaskar spoke with a level voice, but Hunter detected the underlying tension.

"We have to make certain you are still Jnaar."

"What else would we be?"

"Creatures of the Dark Goddess."

"We are not. My mate passed the test," Raaskar protested.

"She may have, but you haven't. Neither have the humans. All four of you will take part in the trial and all four of you must convince us you have not been turned into beasts."

"What kind of trial?"

"You will find out." His gaze rested on Laneea and Raas-ini. "We give you permission to go to your dwelling." Then he added, "We may call upon you again."

Laneea took one step forward. "May I speak?"

"You may."

"Raaskar is my mate and I know with certainty he is who he says he is. We have had no contact with the Shadow-dwellers since we left this city for the hunt."

The old Jnaar allowed himself a tiny smile. "I have no doubt you believe what you say is true, but you have no way to prove it. Your mind may also have been altered and filled with false memories. The Shadow-dwellers are deceitful and smart. They have retained the knowledge of our ancestors and with the help of the Dark Goddess they use it to create strange and different creatures. These humans may be one of those new creations."

"I can assure you they are not," Laneea said. "We've been in their dwelling. It is full of marvels and wonderful things. They have light brighter than the fire-rocks and they control when the light shines and when it is dark. It is warm and dry inside their giant egg that rests on the snow and it can withstand the strongest winds. I've seen images of the world they come from and it is different from Iceworld. On their home world, they live on the surface and don't hide underground the way we do at the time of palos."

"That is enough chattering from this female," the first Inquisitor thundered. He looked at the lead-guard. "Take the males away."

When the guards moved toward them, Hunter glanced at Malone's grim face and noticed his white knuckles on the laser he clutched to his body. "Don't do anything foolish, Malone," he hissed.

"What do they want from us?" the big man asked, not even trying to keep his voice down.

"We'll have to pass a test," Hunter said, "I don't know what kind of test, though. Just stay calm."

The lead-guard approached Malone and gave him a push. "Move," he ordered.

Malone, of course, didn't understand him. He pushed back, growling like an enraged Keeras. When the guard lifted his spear, Malone kicked it out of his hand and punched him in the face. As the guard went down, the other five moved in, spears high.

"Stay back!" Hunter thundered in the Jnaar language, cursing Malone silently. Then he burned a hole into the floor with his laser.

The guards stopped, surprised by either the blinding spear of light from Hunter's weapon or by his sudden command of their language. Hunter aimed his rifle at the three old men behind the table.

"Let's stop this nonsense right now," he said in a sharp voice. "What I hold in my hands is a weapon, much superior to your puny spears or bows. I could kill you all with just one sweep, but I won't. We came in peace, looking for one of our own. We have no desire to harm anyone. Raaskar is our friend. He assured us we'd be welcome in your city, so don't make a liar out of him."

"You speak our language?" one of the Inquisitors said with a quavering voice.

"I speak and understand your language," Hunter told him. "Order your guards to put their spears onto the floor. After that we'll walk out of here unmolested. We will go with Raaskar and his family. You will tell your people everything is fine. We are not your enemies and we are not creatures of this Dark Goddess. Raaskar said you were a peaceful race. I hope that is so." He smiled grimly. "Unfortunately, humans are not peaceful, but we try to be. If any harm comes to us, our people will come and avenge our deaths. The carnage would be terrible."

The old man looked from Hunter to Raaskar. "This human says you are his friend?"

Raaskar nodded. "That is true. He is my friend."

"He does not act friendly," the old Jnaar observed. "He seems enraged and more savage than a Sras warrior."

"That is because he and his companions are trained warriors and they reacted to a threat. You threatened them. Even though they are fierce warriors, they will not harm anyone if the threat is lifted. I will vouch for them."

Hunter relaxed, smiling to himself. Raaskar was certainly a glib liar and a smooth talker. Malone was the only trained warrior among them and, feeling secure in his abilities as a fighter, he had allowed himself to lose his temper, creating a situation that could have ended horribly.

The three Inquisitors put their heads together and whispered to each other. After a few moments one of them spoke. "We are in agreement. You have passed the test. There will be no further inquiries made." His purple eyes searched out Hunter. "We are a peaceful people and we do not wish to enter into a conflict with the humans. We have enough problems with the Sras and the Shadow-dwellers."

"We did not come here to add to your problems. As Raaskar already told you, we came here to ask for your help in locating one of our females. She was taken underground by what appeared to be Jnaar riding Heeskas."

"We are not aware of anyone brought here, but the tunnels lead to many cities. She could have been taken to one of those. We will lend you assistance in finding your mate if you will guarantee us that your people will never attack or invade us."

"I can give you that guarantee. We have no desire to invade any of your cities." Hunter smiled. "The female we search is not my mate."

The Inquisitor pulled his thin lips into a partial smile. "I assumed she was since you put yourself into danger to find one female. She must be very important."

"Every person in our tribe is important. We care for our people and we will search for her until we find her or discover what happened to her."

Seeing movement on the floor, Hunter looked and saw the guard Malone had punched out staggering to his feet. Wiping the blood from his face with a large hand, he gingerly touched his nose and grunted.

Glaring at Malone, he bent to pick up his spear, when one of the Inquisitors bellowed. "Stop! The strangers have been cleared. We have no more need for your services. Go outside and tell everyone to go about their business. There will be no trial."

The guard touched his shoulder with his fist. "As you command, Inquisitor." He gave the other guards a sign with his hand. They picked up their spears and cleared the room.

Heaving a sigh, Hunter shouldered his laser. "I'm glad that's over." He gave Malone a hard stare. "You did a stupid thing, Malone. I warned you to stay calm."

"You should thank your lucky stars I did what I did," Malone growled.

"I'm thanking my lucky stars it turned out this way. We could all be dead now."

"Well, we're not. Sometimes you have to act and not talk. I'm a soldier not a politician. I don't waste time talking."

Glancing at the three old Jnaar, Hunter did not miss the keen interest they showed in the exchange between him and Malone. "We'll discuss this at another time, Malone," he said under his breath.

He turned his attention back to the Inquisitors. "Any assistance would be greatly appreciated. It will be of mutual benefit to the Jnaar and the humans if our people have a peaceful relationship."

"We agree. Conflict is never a good thing. We will send runners to the nearest cities and see what we can discover. In the meantime, accept our hospitality. We are confident Raaskar will be an excellent host." The Inquisitor looked at Raaskar. "If you are in need of provisions to feed your guests, you have our endorsement to go to the communal storage caves."

Raaskar touched his shoulder. "Thank you, Inquisitor. Do we have permission to take back our weapons?"

"You have."

Raaskar retrieved his bow which leaned in a corner against the wall, while Laneea and Raas-ini picked up their spears. "Come," he said to Hunter.

They followed Raaskar out of the door. There were still quite a few Jnaar assembled outside, curious to get a look at the three strangers. However, their interest had changed from hostility to curiosity. In a way, Hunter was thankful Malone acted the way he did, still wondering and worried what kind of test they would have had to pass. Malone's reckless action may possibly have saved their lives. Of course, he would never tell Malone that.

They left the meeting place behind and turned into a side road. The houses on either side all looked pretty much the same with a few variations. The designs were simple and functional. Hunter doubted that the roofs were waterproof, and they probably wouldn't be suitable for living on the surface of the planet. However, in a closed environment like this they were more than adequate.

Raaskar stopped in front of one of the houses. "Welcome to my home," he said proudly. The door was closed, but Hunter didn't see a lock. Raaskar pushed it open and entered the house. Laneea and Raas-ini walked in after him.

When the humans hesitated to follow them, Raaskar spoke. "You are my guests. Come into my house."

Hunter was the first one to accept his invitation. The interior of the house was dark, but when he walked farther into the room, he saw Laneea and Raas-ini by the windows already pulling back the curtains to let in some light. He noticed furs and pillows fashioned from leather lying on the floor. There was also a low table near one of the windows.

Laneea, in typical female fashion, bent down and started fluffing the pillows, even before she shrugged off her backpack. Raas-ini threw her backpack into one corner and stretched out on one of the furs.

"I'm going to sleep right here," she announced. "I am so tired. I'm happy to be home."

Her mother laughed and knelt beside her. "We are all tired, daughter, and I'm almost inclined to join you." She looked up at Hunter. "Take off your packs and find a place to sit. I cannot offer you any food, but I will go and ask Lan-ini, our oldest daughter, to prepare something to eat for us. She lives in the house next to ours."

"Thank you for your kind offer," Hunter said. "I didn't know you had another daughter, but I couldn't help overhearing when Raaskar talked to his brother that you have two younger sons. Where are they?"

Laneea laughed happily. "They are living with Lan-ini and her mate. His name is Ruuro. You will meet all of them." She rose. "I'm going to speak to Lan-ini and to our sons."

Raaskar nodded. "I will show our guests their room."

Chapter Thirteen

Lan-ini turned out to be as beautiful as her mother and her sister, which did not come as a surprise to Hunter. Her mate, Ruuro, though was a surprise. Tall and massive, he was the biggest Jnaar Hunter had ever seen.

Raaskar didn't miss Hunter's curious stares. "Ruuro's ancestors were a specially bred class of warriors, as were Laneea's," he explained. Then he chuckled softly, "You may have noticed the faint markings on Raas-ini's skin—the signs of a true warrior. She inherited them from her mother's mother. I'm sure she told you about that."

Hunter knew the markings could only be seen when she was naked and then only if one looked closer. "She told me about her ancestry." He took care his expression betrayed nothing. So Raaskar knew about him and Raas-ini, as he suspected all along.

One of the sons, Rasar, was a younger version of Raaskar. Hunter guessed his age to be around fifteen in Earth years, while the youngest, Ruusar, was a couple of years younger. He appeared to take after Laneea with more delicate features and finer bones.

Lan-ini, with the help of her mother and younger sister, had prepared a large pot of stew. Hunter recognized the meat. He had eaten similar stew the first time the humans met a tribe of Jnaar. The meat came from the Thrall, the deer-like animals that populated the prairies of Iceworld and, according to Raaskar, even lived in these underground caverns. Hunter was hungry, and the stew tasted great.

"One thing I have to admit," Malone said around a mouthful of stew, "these people may be primitive but they know how to cook spicy food."

"The bread doesn't taste bad either," Cameron said.

They were sitting outside on cushions around low tables, which looked similar to the one they had seen in the building that housed the Inquisitors. There had not been enough room inside the house for so many people, so they decided to eat outside. It was warm and pleasant with no bugs or sudden rain to worry about. As Raaskar informed them, the weather and temperature was always the same in the caverns.

The boys were happy and ecstatic to see their parents and sister again after such a long absence. Everyone had assumed they perished in the harsh winter, and they listened with great interest when Raaskar talked about how he, Laneea, and Raas-ini survived the hostile environment outside. Neither of the boys had ever left the underground world and they couldn't wait for the day when they were old enough to accompany a party of hunters and gatherers into the outside world.

They were in awe when Raaskar described the size of a Krill and made Hunter tell them how he managed to shoot such a majestic giant bird out of the sky. It surprised them that only Hunter spoke the language of the Jnaar and they pitied Cameron and Malone because they couldn't take part in the conversation. Just like any human boys, they were interested in the weapon that threw a spear of white fire, but neither Hunter nor his companions were foolish enough to demonstrate how the lasers worked.

"Why do you have such black skin?" Ruusar, the youngest, said to Hunter.

Amused by the question, Hunter smiled. "Why do you have such white skin?"

Ruusar shrugged. "I was born this way."

Hunter laughed. "So was I."

"Are there many like you?"

"If millions are many, yes, then I'd say there are many like me. On the planet where I was born almost everyone has dark skin, but people of dark color live on other planets also."

"Can I touch you?"

"You must learn to control your curiosity," his mother chided him.

"I only want to know what his skin feels like."

Hunter held out his arm. "Go ahead, touch it. I don't mind."

The young boy touched his arm. "It feels just like mine," he said, almost disappointed.

"What did you expect?" Raas-ini asked her brother.

"I don't know. Something different, like hot or cold, perhaps rough like the skin of a Larroth." Ruusar still wasn't satisfied. "What's that thing on your wrist? It has tiny specks of light that blink sometimes."

"This?" Hunter held up his wrist. "It helps me remember things."

"How?"

That kid wouldn't give up. How could he explain an electronic instrument to a savage? He wouldn't understand a word. If he told him Dawn was self-aware, it would sound like magic to him. Of course, his father, mother, and sister had been exposed to human technology and they didn't freak out.

"I talk to it and it remembers my words. When I need the information, I ask for it and it gives me that."

"Does that thing talk to you?"

"It does."

"Let me hear it talk."

Hunter looked at Raaskar for help, but the older Jnaar had been following the conversation with great interest. Hunter remembered that neither Raaskar nor Laneea or Raas-ini had ever heard or seen him use his computer. He sighed and accepted the inevitable, hoping it wouldn't be a mistake.

"You heard him, Dawn," Hunter addressed the device. "Say something."

"Hello, Ruusar," Dawn said. "I am happy to meet you."

Everyone was suddenly silent and stared at Hunter's wrist. Lan-ini made a sign in the air and whispered a few words. Her mother smiled, as if amused by something.

Raaskar chuckled suddenly. "Your mother and I lived inside the giant egg with the humans and we've seen many wondrous things. Even though I have never heard that bracelet around Hunter's wrist speak, I don't believe there is anything mysterious about it, although it appears to be magic. Always remember our ancestors controlled magic, too."

"But how can it speak? It is too small for someone to hide inside," Ruusar argued.

Raaskar looked at Hunter, clearly expecting some kind of explanation.

"I am very tiny," Dawn answered for Hunter, giving a little laugh. "I don't need much room."

Ruusar bent forward to speak directly to the blinking wrist band. "Can I see you?"

"No," Hunter spoke sharply.

"You heard him," Dawn said. "I cannot show myself to you because I must obey his command."

The boy gave Hunter an astonished look. "Is she your prisoner?"

"She is not my prisoner." Hunter tried to keep his voice level, annoyed at Dawn for playing her little game. "She doesn't have a physical body because she is not a real person."

"She said she is tiny, which means she must have a body," Ruusar insisted.

"Not a real one, believe me," Hunter said patiently.

"I don't understand this." Ruusar shook his head, his gaze fixed on Hunter's wrist as if expecting to see a tiny figure appear.

"Exactly," Hunter said. "You don't understand. Don't feel bad, many humans don't understand the gadgets we use daily, either. We know how to use them, but don't know how they work. That's just the way things are." His eyes met Raaskar's. "You son is very inquisitive. You must be proud of him."

The older Jnaar smiled. "You are correct, I am proud. Sometimes he is a little too inquisitive and it gets him into trouble. Laneea's father's father was a seeker of knowledge. Ruusar inherited his thirst for learning things." He turned his head to look at Raas. "My oldest son is not driven to find out about why things are a certain way. He is more practical. Instead of wondering and questioning why, he acts. He's a warrior and hunter, like me."

"There is nothing wrong with trying to solve problems and thinking about them," Hunter said, giving the young boy an encouraging smile. "Of course, sometimes you have to get your hands dirty and get something done. That's why we need young men like Ruusar and Raas. You are lucky, Raaskar, for having sons like that."

"How about daughters?" Raas-ini asked. "Are we important too?"

Hunter knew she was mocking him. He grinned. "Daughters have their place. I've seen you carry a spear, which means you know how to use it. You survived in the harsh time of palos standing side by side with your father defending yourself and your injured mother against ferocious animals. I have no doubt you're a capable hunter."

Her gaze moved from Hunter to her father's face. "I have hunted with you, father. Am I a capable hunter?"

"You are as skilled a hunter as your mother and I am proud of you, my daughter," Raaskar said. "Not only are you a great hunter, you are also a warrior, as good as any male, and it does not come as a surprise, since you have inherited the genes of your mother's ancestors. I would not hesitate to have you guard my back against our enemies in battle."

Raas-ini was visibly pleased by her father's answer. Her purple eyes glittered with pride when she looked at Hunter. "You heard my father. I can hunt and fight as good as any male. But there are many sides to me. I can be as gentle as a newborn Thrall or as fierce as an enraged Keeras."

"I have no doubt," Hunter said. Images of her naked body writhing above him appeared unbidden. As gentle and as fierce as she was in her lovemaking with a temper to match.

"All this talk about hunting and battling," Lan-ini said. "I have no interest in either. I leave the hunting and fighting to Ruuro. I'd rather clean the skins he brings home and work them into soft leather so I can make clothes to cover our bodies." She pointed to a row of various shapes of pottery lined up on a patch of gravel. "Those are the other things I'm interested in. Making beautiful jugs."

"I guess you're the artist in the family," Hunter said. "You seem to be gifted with your hands."

"Lan-ini has been kissed by the gods." Laneea looked at her oldest daughter with pride. "She makes many beautiful things. She has many talents."

"One of them being a good cook." Hunter held up his bowl, which was also made from clay. "Do you still have some stew left?"

Lan-ini laughed, obviously pleased with Hunter's praise. "There is plenty left." She got up and went into the house. Coming back with a small pot she filled up his bowl.

"I'll have some more," Malone said, holding up his bowl.

Lan-ini gave him a smile and put a ladle full of stew into his bowl. "It seems you like it too. That makes me happy."

Malone looked at Hunter. "What did she say?"

"She's happy you like her stew."

"Oh." Malone beamed. "Tell her it's the best stew I've ever eaten."

"Best stew he ever ate," Hunter translated.

Laughing, Lan-ini gave Malone another portion. "He's a big male. He probably eats a lot of food." With a look at Cameron, she said, "How about your companion? Is he still hungry?"

Cameron picked up his empty bowl from the table and held it up. After she filled it, he said, "Stosa," which meant thank you.

She gave him a surprised look and touched her chest. Loosely translated the gesture meant "you're welcome. I am pleased."

"I thought he didn't speak our language," she said to Hunter.

"He doesn't, but he's trying to learn it." He wondered how much Cameron understood. Dawn transferred everything she learned about the Jnaar language into his computer and had been teaching him in his sleep every night. He might not be able to speak the language, but he should understand a lot.

Hunter felt a soft hand on his shoulder. When he turned his head and looked up, he saw Raas-ini standing behind him.

She held a cup in her hand and offered it to him. "You must be thirsty," she said.

Surprised, he took the cup from her. "Yes, I am. What are you offering me?"

"It is juice from the fruit of the dylian-tree." Her smile seemed impish. "We drink it only on special occasions."

"And this is a special occasion?"

"It is. We celebrate our safe return home." Her hand lingered on his shoulder for another moment and then she walked away and took her place at the end of the table across from him.

He shook his head, curious what that was all about. Ever since their sexual encounter that first night, she had spoken to him only briefly, ignoring him most of the time. He didn't know why she gave him the cold shoulder and he wondered now about the sudden change in her behavior.

Sniffing the liquid in the cup, he smelled a fruity aroma. When he tasted it he found it pleasant if slightly acidic, but otherwise sweet and smooth. It went down easy, almost like a gentle, sparkling wine. Only after he emptied his fourth cup did he realize the liquid had also contained a high percentage of alcohol… and something that went straight to his penis. He suddenly felt horny.

Cameron and Malone seemed to be in good spirits too, and he wondered if they were horny as well. He didn't know if it was his imagination, but he got the impression Raas-ini had been watching him throughout the meal. It seemed as soon as his cup was empty she was there with her jug to fill it up again. When she saw him looking at her, she gave him a sweet smile.

All the adult Jnaar were laughing a lot and also drinking their fair share. Ruuro went into the house and got a long tube with a row of holes running down its length. When he began blowing into it Hunter realized it was a flute. He had not expected the big savage to produce such beautiful music. After a while the women sang along. He and the others sat listening to the songs, enchanted by the haunting melodies and the pleasing voices of the three women.

Hunter tried to make out the words they sang and realized the songs told the stories of the Jnaar's past. They were ballads of heroes from another time, of adventures on other worlds.

After they stopped singing, everyone sat in silence, including the humans.

"That was beautiful," Malone said into the silence. "I wish I had understood the words. Who would have thought savages could make such wonderful music."

"The words were as beautiful as the music. You would have liked them. Besides, these people may be savages, but the Jnaar are an old race, much older than humanity. These songs give you a glimpse into their history." Hunter looked up when he saw Raas-ini approaching him.

She sat down beside him and touched his arm. "We just told you the story of our people," she said softly. "Perhaps someday you can tell me about yours."

He chuckled. "I would never be able to tell it the way you did. I don't play a musical instrument and I'm afraid my voice is better suited to shouting than singing."

"Then you can shout it to me." She laughed and leaned against him. "Come and walk with me. I want to show you my city." She rose and pulled him with her.

"Are you going somewhere, Hunter?" Cameron called after them.

"Just for a walk. I think I need to clear my head," Hunter told him.

"Shouldn't you take a weapon?"

"I'll be fine. We'll have to show these people our good will."

"Well, be careful."

They walked down the road, not talking much. Once in a while Raas-ini pointed at one of the houses they passed and told him who lived there. After a few turns they were at the meeting place. Hunter recognized the building with the barred windows. He also saw something he hadn't noticed when they were taken into that building to be interrogated. It seemed to be part of a window above the entrance doors and it looked suspiciously like a clock.

"What is that?" he asked Raas-ini, indicating the object of his interest.

"That is the time-counter."

"What exactly does it do?"

"It counts the time," she said, laughing.

"I don't understand. Can you explain it in more detail?"

She shrugged with an apologetic smile. "I don't understand it, but I'll tell you what little I know. When our ancestors came to this world, they kept track of the light and dark periods, and of the number of winters. They had machines that did that for them. Those machines were kept alive by the light outside, but when they moved into the tunnels and caverns, the machines didn't work anymore, so they built simple machines that needed to be tended by the Timekeepers. One of them sits in the room behind the time counter and guards it. He makes sure it never stops running."

Hunter nodded, realizing she was describing a clock. It made sense the Jnaar would have instruments to keep track of days, years, and the passing of time in general. Intelligent beings develop math and they count. They also keep records.

He lifted his left arm and touched the gadget on his wrist. "Your brother wanted to know what this is. I told him it helps me remember things, but it does more than that. It also keeps track of light and dark and of the seasons on the outside. Since it is always light in these caverns, this will tell me when it's time to sleep and when it's time to be awake." He glanced at the crystal, giving Dawn the silent command to display the time. "According to this we should be sleeping now."

She smiled. "According to the sirril flowers the time for sleeping has not arrived yet." She showed him a bed of red flowers growing in front of the building with the clock. "When those flowers close, we will sleep. Everybody knows that. The sirril plants grow in abundance everywhere."

"I remember you father telling me about those plants. I didn't quite understand how exactly it worked. Do they close and open at regular intervals?"

"Yes, they are always consistent."

"Primitive, but it seems to work. It proves again, intelligent beings always find a way to adapt to their environment." Usually it was much easier for savages than for civilized people. He decided to keep those thoughts to himself. He didn't want to hurt Raas-ini's feelings. She didn't think of herself as a savage.

There were a few Jnaar still in the meeting place walking or sitting on small benches. They didn't appear to pay any attention to him and Raas-ini, but he knew they were watching them. He was a stranger, different from them, and it was only natural they'd be curious.

Raas-ini steered him down another street. "Where are we going?" he asked.

"I want to show you my special place," she said.

Just before they turned into the new street, two young Jnaar males came out of one of the houses. When they saw Hunter and Raas-ini, one of them raised a hand.

"Raas-ini."

She stopped walking and waited for him to approach her.

"You are back," he said, obviously surprised to see her.

"Yes, I am," she replied.

"We thought you were lost and would never come back."

"You thought wrong, Maararas. We survived."

When he looked at Hunter, his face seemed to cloud over. "Who is the stranger you brought to our city?"

"This is Hunter," she said. "He and his people saved us and gave us shelter."

"Are there more like him?"

"Yes."

"He is not from this world."

"No. His people come from far away."

Hunter sensed an air of hostility from the young Jnaar and wished he had taken a weapon after all.

"Why is he with you?" Maararas spoke with a demanding, almost threatening voice. There was no mistaking his resentment toward Hunter.

"He is my guest. Besides, the reason he is with me does not concern you." Her tone was cool, but Hunter detected an underlying unease about her, as if she were trying to convince herself that everything was normal.

"I will come and talk to your father about us," he told her, and then he turned and walked away.

Hunter looked after him. "Who is he?" He wondered if he actually wanted to know.

"I was supposed to be his mate," she said, confirming something he had already guessed.

"And now?"

Her hand squeezed his arm. "Now? Now there is you." She pulled him with her. "Let's not talk about Maararas."

He wanted to ask her questions but decided against it. He had not thought there might be a potential mate waiting for her. It never came up. They walked in silence for a while. He realized they had left the residential area. There weren't any houses on either side of the road, only trees and shrubs.

"Down this way," Raas-ini said and turned into a narrow trail. He walked behind her, wondering where they were headed. The gurgling sound of running water made him guess it might be a creek. His guess was correct. The trail ended abruptly to reveal a small pond fed by a narrow brook.

"Not many come here," Raas-ini said. "Everyone goes to the large pool, which is deeper and the water is warmer. This water is cold but clean and fresh."

She undid her top and removed it, exposing her small breasts. Then she slipped out of her kilt.

"Don't you want to wash your body?"

"Didn't you say the water was cold?"

She came close and tugged on his shirt. "I will make you warm after bathing."

Grabbing her, he drew her to him. "I thought you wanted nothing to do with me. Seeing Maararas made me wonder even more. What changed your mind?"

"I realized I love you after all. We will work out our differences." She kissed him fiercely. Breaking the kiss, she panted, "Let's cool off after. Right now, I need to feel your big, black pleasure stick inside me."

He didn't need any encouragement. The walk had done nothing to calm his extreme desire for her. His penis was painfully stiff inside his pants, and he couldn't wait to shove it into her hot pussy.

Pushing his pants down to his ankles, she knelt in front of him. Fondling his hard member, she flicked a warm tongue over its tip. Wrapping her lips around the slippery head, she sucked him gently. He closed his eyes, enjoying her gentle tonguing. When she sucked him deep into her mouth, he groaned loudly and grabbed her head. Not wanting to come already, he eased his penis out of her and pulled her upright.

Holding her tight, he sank to his knees and laid her onto her back. Her legs parted willingly and he fell between them. His aching penis found her thick labia and then he slid with ease into her warm and creamy sheath.

She cried out as he pushed deep into her and dug her fingers into his biceps. "You feel so big inside me," she moaned. "Have you grown?"

"It must be the substance you put into my drink," he grunted.

Her laugh came out as a gag. "How did you know?" she panted.

"It's not the first time I drank an alcoholic drink, but I never got this horny from one."

Holding her gyrating buttocks in his hands, he moved with powerful strokes between her widespread thighs. She whimpered loudly, throwing her head from side to side.

"Don't stop," she nearly screamed. "Don't ever stop!"

He didn't stop for a long time. While he was moving in and out of her quaking pussy, he realized whatever she put into his wine gave him incredible stamina and created almost unbelievable pleasure. It radiated from his genital area throughout his whole body. She must have taken the same stuff, because she clawed his back with stiff fingers and bleated like a wounded fawn, hammering her slim body up against his.

When he couldn't hold back any longer, he crushed her to him and erupted inside her. He thought his rampant penis would never stop gushing. Every throb was more powerful than the one before. The gushing stopped, but the heavenly rapture stayed with him, and he closed his eyes to concentrate on the pure pleasure searing every fiber of his body.

There didn't seem to be enough air to fill his wheezing lungs as he lay shuddering in her embrace. He could hear her gasping and felt the heaving of her chest against his like a giant thudding heart.

They lay thus for a long time, trying to recuperate from the ordeal they had put their tired bodies through. Both of them finally calmed down and Hunter sighed with regret as the blissful feeling slowly faded away.

Raas-ini stirred under him. "I can't move," she complained.

He rolled from her and lay beside her on his side. "What did you put into the wine?"

She laughed softly. "We call it gurvanni, which means dreamwings. We extract it from the root of the dylian-tree. You need only a small drop in a large jug. Too much could kill you."

"The wine I drank is made from the fruit of the same tree, correct?"

"The dylian-tree has many uses. The dried leaves have healing qualities, and the bark, ground into fine powder, helps to close a bleeding wound."

"I assume chewing the roots kills you?"

She nodded. "Every plant has two sides. One beneficial and one deadly. One needs to know which part of the plant to use for what purpose."

"You're knowledgeable in the use of plants?"

"Yes, I am. Most of us are. There is danger all around us. We are taught the basic survival skills when we are very young, but some of us, like me, are more interested than others to learn." She sat up. "Let's wash up and go home. I am tired now. It's been a long day."

Raas-ini was the first one to jump into the small pond. Hunter followed her slowly. The water was cold, but he felt grimy, his body slick with perspiration, and the water was refreshing on his hot skin. Raas-ini laughed happily and splashed him. He reached for her and pulled her close. Her breasts rested against his chest, soft and warm.

Looking at him with her large eyes, she smiled and put her arms around him. "Did I tell you that I love you?"

"You did. I love you, too." He kissed her gently, realizing it was the heat of the moment and the aftereffects of the drug both had consumed to make them say those words. How could they love each other? They had evolved from totally different origins. Her ancestors were probably reptiles hiding in the swamps looking for prey while his climbed the trees looking for safety. The females of her species laid eggs. Human women bore live young. That bridge could never be crossed. They were not compatible and that was the cold fact.

Chapter Fourteen

Cameron watched Hunter and the alien girl walking away with misgivings. Hunter was their liaison's officer. He was the one who was fluent in the Jnaar language and even knowledgeable with many of their customs, but possibly a little too friendly with the daughter of Raaskar. Cameron had discovered them that first night when they camped in the cavern. His Guard-Dog alerted him to movement by the small pond. When he got up to investigate, he saw Hunter moving enthusiastically between Raas-ini's widespread thighs. Both of them were naked, and there was no doubt about what they were doing. Somehow, he hadn't been surprised, because he remembered seeing Hunter and the Jnaar girl together back at the Station. He hoped it would not cause friction between the humans and the Jnaar.

Some parents, especially in more primitive societies, were protective of their young. What if she was already promised to a Jnaar male for a mate? Her parents might not look kindly upon an alien screwing their daughter. Hunter, as chummy as he seemed to be with Raaskar, was an alien and not of their kind.

The Jnaar were friendly enough, but the incident with the Inquisitors gave Cameron pause to think. After all, these people were savages with their own customs and probably a host of taboos. The humans were strangers in this underground city and could not afford to antagonize their hosts. It could mean the difference between staying alive and being murdered.

"Where the hell is Hunter going?" Malone demanded with a lowered voice. He seemed to have difficulty formulating the words because of all the wine he had consumed.

Cameron could feel the alcohol go to his own head and limbs. He gave the big man a sarcastic chuckle.

"Probably to a quiet place to fuck her. Haven't you noticed how he's been undressing her with his eyes for the past hour or so? Like a horny lovesick puppy."

"I didn't miss the way she hovered over him with that jug of wine, filling up his cup every time it was empty. As if she wanted him to get drunk. You and I didn't get that kind of service." He stared into his cup. "I could use a refill right now."

"Perhaps you shouldn't, Malone. One more cup and you won't be able to talk coherently. We have to keep our wits about us. We're not exactly in a friendly camp, if you know what I mean."

"I wish I could understand what they're talking about," the big man complained. "Are they plotting to murder us in our sleep or are they planning to bring us a couple of young virgins to keep us company for the night." He laughed when Cameron gave him a perplexed look. "You have to admit these Jnaar women are beauties. I've never seen so many hot-looking women in one place on any of the planets I've been."

"The only women you've seen were probably all whores and courtesans. Let me assure you, they aren't plotting our murder, but neither will they be supplying us with any virgins. They're talking about the ordeal Raaskar and his family went through while trying to survive the cold and the snow."

Malone's eyes squinted when he looked at Cameron. "How do you know that?"

There was no need to keep it a secret any longer. "I am able to understand quite a bit of what they're saying."

"I thought you didn't speak their language?"

"I didn't say I can speak the language, I said I can understand them. There is a difference."

"When did you learn?"

Cameron showed him his wrist. "My little computer here. Hunter downloaded everything he had in his wrist-computer's memory into mine and I've been learning the language subliminally. I'm just not sure if I can pronounce the words correctly."

"You'll never know until you've tried."

"You're right. Now is probably as good a time as any. I don't know about you, but I'm dog tired. I wouldn't mind getting a bit of rest now. According to my watch it's past midnight outside." Cameron rose unsteadily to his feet and approached Raaskar.

The Jnaar looked up when he saw Cameron standing beside him.

Cameron cleared his throat, hoping the alien words would come out the right way. "Raaskar, we wonder where we sleep. Tired."

The surprise was clearly visible in Raaskar's face. "You speak Jnaar?"

Cameron nodded. "A little. I learn slow. Not good speaking. Understand much."

The alien man turned to his family. "We must be careful what we say from now on. The humans understand our language." He laughed, obviously enjoying his little joke.

At least that's what Cameron hoped it was. He didn't share Malone's paranoia about the Jnaar possibly cooking up some kind of plot against them.

"I understand Jnaar. My companion no understand."

Raaskar glanced at Malone. "Why not?"

"Because of this. It teach me. Malone no have one." Cameron pointed at the gadget on his wrist.

"Is there a tiny female inside yours too?"

Cameron chuckled. "No, mine no like Hunter's. No tiny female inside."

"You said you wanted to rest? The sirril flowers are still open, which means it is not time to sleep yet."

"The sirril flowers?"

Raaskar indicated a patch of red flowers near the house. "When they close we go to sleep."

"Ingenious. Telling time by a bunch of flowers," Cameron murmured to himself. "Malone and I tired. Like to sleep. Now."

"Laneea will show you where you can sleep."

Laneea, who had been following their conversation, rose from her sitting position. "Come with me," she said to Cameron.

Cameron gave Malone a sign. The big man stood up and swaggered toward Cameron.

"I shouldn't have drunk so much," he rumbled. "That's potent stuff. I'll probably have a hangover tomorrow."

"I warned you not to have that last cup," Cameron reminded him, not feeling sorry for Malone. "I'm not exactly feeling so great myself, and I didn't drink as much as you."

"Did you by any chance happen to see any latrines somewhere? I don't believe these people are sophisticated enough to have washrooms in their houses."

"I'll ask her later." Cameron followed Laneea into her house. She walked to one of the two curtain-covered entrances on the other side of the room they had entered and pulled open the curtain, revealing another room. The floor was covered with thick Keeras-furs.

"You can sleep in here," she told Cameron. Then she walked over to a corner and unrolled one of three bundles lying side by side. It turned out to be a blanket made from tanned animal skins. "Use these to cover your bodies. If you want it dark, close the curtains on the window."

"Stosa, Laneea." Cameron tried to find the right words to tell her they were looking for the latrine. "One other thing. Where do we…?" He didn't know how exactly to say it, so he hunkered down, hoping she'd know what he meant.

Her silvery laughter teased him. "Wait. I will let Rasar take you there." Standing by the main entrance to the house, she called her son. "Rasar."

The boy came into the house a few moments later.

"Show them the Squatting-place," she told her son.

Rasar nodded and looked at Cameron. "Come with me."

Cameron and Malone followed the boy outside. He led them down a narrow path between the houses across the street toward the wall of the cavern. Coming out in an open area, Cameron saw a number of enclosures made from tall reeds lined up near the wall.

"In there," Rasar said.

The two men parted the leather curtain to the entrance of one of the enclosures and walked in. Cameron counted ten cubicles along the back of the enclosure. They were open in the front. Each cubicle had a strong pole between the two walls fastened high enough to make it comfortable to sit on. Underneath the pole the ground revealed a gaping hole. Two of the cubicles were occupied. The two Jnaar males nodded to the humans but said nothing.

"Primitive but workable," Malone said.

"These people don't believe much in privacy," Cameron observed. He spotted a tall basket filled with balls of fluff. "I guess we use those for wiping."

"I wonder where we can wash up after." Malone looked around as if expecting to find a sink with a waterspout.

"Probably outside somewhere."

Cameron's guess was correct. Rasar showed them a long, hollow reed that seemed to originate somewhere near the wall. The water that flowed from it emptied into a small pool. The men washed their hands and faces.

"I have to admit the Jnaar practice safe hygiene. Not all primitive peoples do," Malone said.

"Everything seems to be well organized." Cameron agreed with Malone's observation. "Of course, we must remember, the Jnaar are descendants of stranded space travelers who came from a highly advanced civilization. They may have fallen into savagery and become a low-tech society, but many of their traditions have survived. Their basic way of life probably hasn't changed much."

"The same is probably going to happen to our descendants if we don't find a way off this planet," Malone said.

"I don't doubt that, but we may be luckier than the Jnaar. We're expecting a ship from Earth in four years."

"If they discover what happened to the colonists on Nu-Eden they may not bother looking for anyone on this planet." Malone sounded pessimistic. Unfortunately, Cameron shared his view.

Laneea wasn't in the house and Rasar went back to his sister's house where the rest of his family still celebrated. Cameron heard them laughing. He picked up his backpack and laser and took them into the room Laneea had shown them. He closed the curtain on the window to darken the room and undressed. Wearing only his briefs, he covered himself with the blanket made from skins, suddenly feeling tired to the point of exhaustion. It had been a long day. Malone was already asleep. Wondering briefly if the big man's soft snoring would keep him awake, Cameron closed his eyes.

When he woke up again, it was morning, according to his chronometer. He realized he had slept without waking for nearly eight hours. Malone was still sleeping, so was Hunter, who lay next to Malone, wrapped in his blanket.

Cameron rose silently, picked up his clothing, and walked into the front room. The curtains were drawn, throwing the room into darkness. As he started to get dressed, he saw a shape lying on the pillows, apparently fast asleep. When he looked closer, he recognized Raas-ini, Raaskar's daughter. He realized that she was naked. Her small breasts were clearly visible in the narrow beam of light creeping through a crack in the curtain. One thing these people lacked was modesty.

He quickly finished dressing. Then he carefully opened the front door and stepped outside. His first thought was it's already daylight when he remembered where he was. It was always daylight in the cavern. He noted that the red flowers near the house were closed, which meant everyone was still sleeping.

Taking a reading with his computer, he marked the house so he would be able to find it again, and then he walked down the street, heading in the opposite direction of the meeting place. He didn't want to go back there.

Breathing deeply, he found the air high in humidity. It reminded him of the jungle areas on Nu-Eden. The trees and shrubs looked green and healthy and he wondered how they received enough moisture to stay so fresh. The city was quiet. There didn't seem to be anybody around. It was probably a good time to do some exploring. Nobody would question his presence in this alien city.

After walking for about half an hour, the street took a turn. It also grew narrower. The absence of houses signaled the outskirts of the city. He stopped to orient himself, when he heard the rustling of branches. Turning to search for the origin of the sound, he saw a young Jnaar female stepping out of a narrow trail among the tall shrubs. When she saw him, she smiled and came closer. She didn't seem to be surprised seeing him standing in the street.

She touched her shoulder with a closed fist. "You are one of the three strangers from the outside. I was hoping to meet you."

"Why you want meet me?" Cameron asked, perplexed.

Her smile deepened. "I did not know you spoke our language. I am

151

glad we will be able to communicate."

"I speak little," Cameron said, spreading both hands in apology.

"It is enough. What is your name?"

"My name is Rob Cameron. Yours?"

"You may call me Carini. I will call you Rob."

Cameron gave her a smile, wondering what she wanted from him. "Rob is good. My friends call me Rob."

Her laughter sounded cheerful. "That means I am your friend." Her large eyes studied him with curiosity. "I heard there is one among you with black skin. He speaks the Jnaar language."

"How you know this?"

"My brother told me. He was one of the guards who took you to the Inquisitors. He said you have magic weapons." She looked him over. "Your hands are empty now. Where are your weapons?"

"I left weapon in Raaskar house. I no want hurt anyone. Jnaar people friends no enemy." He struggled with the words, but somehow, he seemed to find it easier to pronounce them.

"That is good. Why are you walking alone on the street at the time of sleeping?"

"I finish sleeping." He looked at her. "Why are you here?"

"To find you." She laughed when he gave her a questioning look. "Do you want me to be your guide and show you around?"

"Yes. I be happy."

"Then come, I will take you where the dylian-trees grow. The fruit of the trees is used to make a strong drink."

He grimaced. "I know. I drank too much last night. My head fuzzy this morning."

"Then you must eat some of the fruit. It will clear your head." She started walking.

Cameron followed her, his eyes on her slim hips, appreciating the sensuous way they swung. He remembered when he was rescued by one of the Xandra's daughters after he got lost in the jungle on Nu-Eden. She had appeared out of nowhere, naked and beautiful, and led him to a place where he could rest. Not for the first time he marveled how closely the Jnaar females resembled the daughters of the Xandra.

Carini waited for him to catch up with her. "We are almost there," she said. Turning into another trail, she pointed. "See the trees with the yellow globes. Those are dylian-trees. They grow wild. All we have to do is pick their fruit." She walked up to one of the trees and plucked a large, yellow globe from a low-hanging branch. She offered it to him.

"Eat this. It will make your head clear."

He took it from her and looked at it. It was covered with fine fuzz. "Eat like this or peel skin?"

"You can eat it either way, but it is best to eat it with the skin. The skin holds healing powers."

He bit into the soft flesh and was surprised by the sweet taste and the amount of juice dripping from the fruit.

Carini laughed when she saw how he enjoyed it. Then she went and picked another one.

"Let's stay here for a while and talk," she said, lowering herself into the soft grass. "Come, sit across from me."

Cameron followed her invitation. Folding his legs under him, he sat opposite her with a feeling of déjà vu. Before the daughter of the Xandra took him back to Alpha Colony, she had picked a fruit similar to this one, except that one had been blue, and she offered it to him with her mouth. It had made him horny and given him unbelievable stamina when they had sex.

Carini sat with her legs crossed. It made Cameron aware again of the fact the Jnaar didn't wear any underwear under their kilt. He tried not to be too obvious when he looked at her exposed sex-organ, and he wondered briefly if she sat in that position on purpose, since she had asked him to sit across from her.

Damn! He was only away for a few days from Valissa and already he was getting turned on by a strange woman. He wondered if there was something in this fruit other than juice and pulp. He'd better watch himself. But maybe he was getting paranoid and beginning to imagine things that weren't there.

"How is your head?"

"My head? Oh, it is good."

"Not fuzzy anymore?"

"Not fuzzy." It was the truth. His head seemed to be clear. He shoved the last of the fruit into his mouth. "Good fruit."

"Yes, it is," she agreed. "Tell me about yourself. The world you come from, are there many of your kind?"

"Yes. Many. Too many. We leave to seek other worlds."

"Why?"

"To make new home for my people."

"There are not many of your people on Iceworld now. Will more come from your world?" The question sounded innocent enough, but Cameron detected more than mere curiosity.

"Iceworld very cold. Not friendly," he said. "Maybe we leave again." If the ship came in four years. Otherwise they might be here forever. For some reason, he didn't think it was a good idea to tell her that.

"The Jnaar came from a faraway world. They stayed and made this world their home. The Sras have lived here for a long time already before the Jnaar came."

"Jnaar have no choice. Stranded here."

She nodded. "That is true." She finished the fruit she'd been nibbling on and leaned forward. "It is the time of palos outside. How do you survive in the cold and the snow? It must be difficult to hunt and find food. Nothing grows for a long time."

"Our home huge. Warm inside. We store food. We survive." He didn't tell her about the food synthesizer. Not because he didn't want to, but because she wouldn't understand how edible food could be produced from none-edible raw materials. Besides, he didn't have the words to explain the principle to her.

"The humans must be very smart. Perhaps you can teach us some of your knowledge."

"Gladly. We exchange knowledge. Jnaar teach us how to survive on Iceworld. We be friends." He wanted to ask how she knew his species was called humans, but then he remembered her brother was one of the guards. He admired her memory and her apparent thirst for knowledge.

She wiped her hands on the grass and rose. She held out a hand for him to grab. "We will go swimming in the water. It will cleanse our bodies."

He let himself be pulled up. She held onto his hand as she walked beside him.

"Do you have a mate?"

"Yes. I have a mate." He was almost reluctant to admit it. "You have a mate?"

She shook her head. "I have no mate."

"You very beautiful. No trouble finding a mate."

She let go of his hand and danced away from him. Waiting for him, she looked at him, her large eyes almost hidden by her long lashes. When he caught up with her, she stood close to him and looked into his face.

"In the eyes of a Jnaar male I am no more beautiful than any of the other females. Do you find me exceptionally beautiful?"

Feeling uncomfortable by her nearness but strangely attracted to her, he fought the impulse to put his arms around her supple body and crush her to him. "I think you are most beautiful."

"Good." She laughed and gave him a quick kiss on the lips. Then she grabbed his hand again and walked.

Startled by the unexpected intimate gesture, he let her pull him along, his feelings in turmoil. This beautiful, alien girl made his head spin and heart race. His loins throbbed. He found himself strangely attracted to her, and he didn't think it was because of the fruit he ate.

He was like a horny teenager who had just been kissed by the girl he has the hots for, but is not allowed to ever touch because she is out of his league. This girl was forbidden fruit. Valissa was the only one he loved.

The trail ended in a small glade with a pond. Everything looked so peaceful and the water inviting. There was barely a ripple on the surface and the water was so clear he could see the white sand at the bottom.

While he stood admiring the view, Carini removed her top and pushed down her leather kilt. Naked, she gave him one of her dreamy looks. Cameron's mind was transported for a second time to Nu-Eden. There had been many such small bodies of water in the jungle, and here he was again by such a pond with an alien girl. With her clothes off, Carini's resemblance to the Xandra's daughters was remarkable and eerie.

She held out a hand to him. "Are you coming with me into the water?" Her large, purple eyes seemed to pull him into their depth and her red lips beckoned.

He closed his eyes for a moment to wipe away the memories of Nu-Eden and to break the spell she had cast over him. Desperately, he tried to conjure up Valissa's face in his mind. When he opened his eyes again,

Carini stood in front of him, concern on her face.

"Are you not feeling well?"

The enchanted moment had passed. He chuckled softly. "I'm fine. Memories from the past."

"Pleasant memories?"

He nodded. "Yes, mostly. Now we go swimming."

"You have to take off your clothing first." Her face was curious again. "Unless your customs don't allow you to be without clothes in front of a stranger."

"We have no customs like that." He grimaced. Except his own stupid hang-ups.

She watched him getting undressed. He was not a prude, not normally, but having a strange, beautiful, naked girl watch while he took off his clothes made him uncomfortable. He might have felt differently if the reason for him getting naked was to have sex with her, but that was not the case at this moment. He was only going for a swim.

Acutely conscious of her eyes on his sex-organ after he pushed down his briefs, he moved toward the pond. He didn't know if she was aware of his discomfort, but she laughed and rushed him. Jumping onto his back, she wrapped her long legs and arms around him. Taken off guard, he lost his balance and tumbled into the water with her clinging to him. Both of them sank below the surface. Expecting cold spring water, he registered unconsciously how pleasantly warm it felt. She released her hold on him and swam away under water. Coming up for air, he shook his head to clear the water out of his eyes.

Her head appeared above the surface a short distance away. He heard her laugh and then she dove again. The clear water distorted her body as she swam toward him, creating the illusion of a large, predatory fish searching for prey. He was the prey.

As she rose in front of him, water dripping from her long hair and running down her lithe body in tiny rivulets, her small solid breasts grazed his chest. Her smile teased him. When he instinctively reached for her, she eluded him easily and slipped from his grasp.

What was he doing? She was playing with him, but he couldn't afford to fall for her attempts to seduce him, if she was trying to do that. He was a stranger among aliens and he didn't know their customs. Perhaps this is just a little game she was playing out of boredom. Why would she wander around at this time of their night unless she was bored?

Floating on her back, she drifted away from him, exposing the front of her body to his eyes. Her genital area was bare of any pubic hair, something he couldn't help but notice. Another reminder how much the Jnaar females looked like the daughters of the Xandra on Nu-Eden. He remembered Miller telling him about alien space travelers who had come to Nu-Eden centuries ago. They called their race Genaar. He hadn't really believed Miller's story, but he knew now that it was true. The Jnaar on Iceworld were of the same race as the Genaar on Nu-Eden. Their ancestors were stranded on both planets a thousand year ago.

According to Miller, the Genaar were the first alien race the Xandra encountered and she learned a lot from them. When she created her daughters, she made them in the image of the Genaar females.

Carini swam back to him. "You want me to scrub your back?"

At first, he wanted to say no, but then he nodded. What harm could it do if he let her rub his back?

She moved behind him and splashed him with water. Then she ran her hands down his back slowly and with gentle pressure. He closed his eyes, enjoying the feel of her soft hands on his skin. Even though he tried to suppress it, he couldn't stop his penis from swelling. There was something about Carini that caused his body to react when she was near.

If she noticed, she didn't comment. She hummed a little tune, acting as if stroking a stranger's back and shoulders with the gentle touch of a lover was the most natural thing for her to do.

She was an alien. Perhaps they did this sort of thing as a sign of hospitality. He wasn't really cheating on Valissa.

He knew what he told himself was only an excuse to justify the pleasure he experienced being touched so intimately by a strange woman.

She stopped. "Now you wash me."

He turned around. She stood in front of him with a wicked little smile. "The front first."

He scooped up water with his cupped hands and dribbled it on her chest. Then he washed her shoulders and her arms. She pushed out her breasts. "Don't forget these."

Putting his hands on her breasts, he rubbed them gently with circular motions. She moaned and closed her eyes.

"That feels nice."

He moved one hand down to her flat belly and realized she didn't have a navel. He hadn't noticed it before.

He remembered what Raaskar told them when they walked down the main road after entering this city. He had pointed out a large pond. "The next generation of eggs will hatch in there." He hadn't understood the meaning of Raaskar's words at the time.

Now it made sense. The Jnaar females laid eggs. There was no need for an umbilical cord. It also meant if he had sex with her, she wouldn't get pregnant. At least that's what he assumed.

When he touched the bulging mound of her femininity, she gave another moan and pressed her lower body against his probing fingers. Encouraged by her reaction, he found her slit and rubbed it gently. She felt slippery and he inserted a finger into her pussy, moving it in and out. Gasping loudly, she opened her eyes but kept her lids half-closed. Her hand snaked forward and then he felt her warm fingers on his erection.

"Finally, you understand what I wanted from you all along," she whispered.

His penis was as hard as iron in her soft hand and he groaned. "I also want," he said harshly, "but do not know if I can."

"You can," she said, her lips smiling, her hand squeezing him.

"You no understand. My mate…"

She stopped him by pressing her lips against his and kissing him with great passion. She tasted as sweet as the fruit she had consumed.

"Your mate is not here. She will not know. I am here."

He put his arms around her and cupped her buttocks with his hands. She lifted her legs and wrapped them around his torso. He felt his stiff member grabbed by her thick pussy lips and then she sheathed him. She was tight but soft and yielding. Moving her buttocks in his hands, she milked him with vigorous movements. He lost his balance and they both tumbled under water. She still clung to him and kept on snapping her pelvis back and forth, but he let go of her buttocks and they separated.

Laughing, she surfaced and grabbed his arm. "Let's go on land where it is safer."

Scrambling out of the water, she moved to a spot near one of the trees and lay down, her legs open in invitation. He knelt between her spread thighs and, lifting her lower body, he pulled her closer. Then he entered her again. Holding on to her slim hips, he enjoyed the way the muscles of her flat belly rippled as she twisted her supple body like a boneless snake in front of him. The gaze of his eyes fastened on her breasts. He admired their perfect shape and the way they moved on her fast-rising chest. They seemed suddenly larger than he remembered.

Grabbing his arms, she pulled her body up and sat in his lap, her lower body still rotating with frenzied movements. She smiled and put her arms around him. Then she kissed him deeply, sucking on his tongue.

"Do all males of your people have so much hair covering their face?"

"No," he said, "but some do."

"Why?"

"No real reason. We just like it."

"It tickles my lips," she said. Then she kissed him again.

He put her onto her back. Lying on top of her, he fucked her slowly with long, deep strokes for a long time, bringing her to several orgasms. She knew how to keep him from coming too soon by pressing a finger against the root of his scrotum whenever he thought he couldn't hold it any longer.

The pleasure surging through his body was constant. Her sheath flowed freely the whole time and supplied the lubrication necessary to keep her from drying up.

When he finally exploded inside her, she doused him with her warm fluid as she reached her own powerful climax. His loud grunts blended with her soft whimpers, and their bodies shuddered violently in each other's arms as they rode the crest of the greatest physical joy a man and a woman can ever experience. The fact that the woman in his arms was from a different species did not diminish the rapture of her embrace. Instead, it enhanced the nearly unbearable pleasure he found.

Breathing harshly, Cameron rolled onto his back and closed his eyes for a moment. Lying beside Carini, he listened to her little gasps as she tried to fill her lungs with air. He was perspiring profusely, and when he turned to look at her, he noticed the slick sheen on her smooth skin.

As if reading his mind, she laughed softly. "I think we need to wash again."

"I agree."

The water felt refreshing on their hot bodies. They washed each other and Cameron was strangely satisfied and happy. Right at this moment, he didn't want to think about Valissa and gave all of his attention to the alien woman who made him feel this way. What just happened meant nothing. He was not in love with Carini and she didn't love him. A chance encounter of two lonely people had led to an hour of hot and passionate lovemaking. That was all there was to it. At least that's what he told himself.

When they climbed back on land, he saw a couple of the same small, cat-like animals they had seen with Raaskar's brother. They stood looking at Cameron with their luminous, yellow eyes, as if studying him.

"What are those?" he asked Carini. "Are they dangerous?"

"No, the Sreel are not dangerous. Not to us. The hunters use them for tracking, but these are guardians who patrol the valley to warn us against intruders." She held out a hand to them. One of them came closer and sniffed it. The other one kept its distance, still studying Cameron.

"They look intelligent," he observed. "They're watching me."

"They are smart, and they are watching you," Carini agreed. "You are a stranger, but they know you are with me. Next time they see you they'll ignore you."

The one that had sniffed Carini's hand came to him and sniffed his leg. It seemed satisfied and went back to its companion. Then both animals disappeared among the shrubs.

Carini put on her clothes. After she was dressed, she came and stood in front of him. Putting her arms around his neck, she looked into his eyes.

"I gave my body to you out of free will and you gave your body to me. From now on there is a bond between us. Next time we meet we won't be strangers anymore but friends, Rob Cameron."

She kissed him and then she slipped away. Before he could say something, she was gone. He could still feel his lips tingling from her kiss and wished she hadn't left this suddenly. Dressing slowly, he seemed to come out of some kind of spell he had been under.

What the hell happened here? Did he dream this or did he just have one of the best fucks of his life?

Looking around, he had no idea where he was. There was no sun and there were no stars he could use to guide him. He remembered taking a reading when he left Raaskar's home. Running his fingers over the crystal on his wrist-computer, he brought up the three-dimensional map it had created. It showed his present position, and he realized it was actually easy to find his way. All he had to do was walk back the way he came.

After one last look at the pristine water of the pond, he headed for home.

THE END

The adventure continues in The Xandra, Book Eight, available soon from Melange Books

Chapter One

"They've been gone nearly a month," Valissa said. "I wish Rob had stayed here. I miss him and feel lonesome without him. He said they'd try to send messages, but he didn't think it was possible. The rocks would probably prevent any signals from getting through."

"It seems he was right about that since we haven't heard from them." Teresa put her hand over Valissa's in a gesture of friendship. "Don't worry so much. I'm sure they're okay." She gave Valissa an encouraging smile. "You're not alone. I'm here for you and so is Holger."

Valissa wiped her nose with the back of her hand and sniffed. "I know and I appreciate it, but you can't replace Rob when I sleep alone in my bed at night."

"I'm alone at night also, honey. Too bad that big hunk of a man, you know who I'm talking about, was so damned reserved. Who would have thought a man like that has so many inhibitions. I would have given him a good time." Teresa laughed heartily. "He would have remembered my great passion as he's sleeping in those dark, cold tunnels without a woman embracing his hard, muscular body."

Schreiber snickered. "I'm glad I don't have all these sexual hang-ups. Must be a drain on your system."

"Well, Holger, my friend, somehow I can't believe that you don't have any sexual desires. You can't be dead down there, and I don't really want to know how you relieve your anxieties, which I have no doubt you have. So you're not attracted to women. You like men. Tell me, did you ever have the hots for another man?"

"I had. A long time ago." He seemed reluctant to answer her.

"Can't be that long ago. You're not so old. Was he your lover?"

Schreiber nodded, a faraway look in his dark eyes. "For a short time only."

"Did you have a sexual relationship with him?" Teresa sounded almost like an interrogator. When Schreiber didn't answer, she asked again. "Did you?"

"What do you think?" Schreiber's eyes flashed angrily.

His reaction surprised Valissa. She had never seen him angry. He was usually calm and in control of his emotions.

If Teresa noticed his sudden irritation, she didn't show it. She slapped his shoulder with a jovial laugh. "So you did have a little taste of heaven, you sly dog. Perhaps if the right man came along you would discover feelings you thought were dead. That's how I felt with Malone, believe it or not. He may look like a huge ogre to you, but I found him ruggedly handsome."

"Why didn't you tell him that?" Schreiber seemed to have regained his composure. "You have nobody to blame but yourself if you feel like you've missed having his sweaty body laboring on top of yours."

"You make it sound like something dirty. I call it making passionate love."

"Call it what you will. You should have made the first move when you noticed he didn't have the guts to romance you." Schreiber took a swig from his coffee mug. "Now you may never get the chance."

"Why shouldn't I?"

"He may get lost in those underground tunnels and not come back."

"Don't be so negative!" Teresa chided him and made a motion with her head toward Valissa. "Of course he'll be back. They'll all come back safe and sound."

"And soon," Valissa said. "I hope they find that woman, otherwise it'll all have been for nothing." She rose from her seat. "See you at lunch. I'm going to do my exercises." She smiled at them. "I don't want to be fat and out of shape when Rob comes back."

"No chance of that happening, unless you get yourself pregnant by one of the men who have been ogling you and who would like nothing better than to get into those tight pants you're wearing. You eat like a bird and spend most of your time in the exercise room." Teresa heaved a loud sigh. "I wish I had the drive and the desire to be so disciplined." She touched her belly. "I have to get rid of this little ring I've noticed lately. I wish I had a man to exercise with. It's so much more fun."

Holger shook his head. "Like I said—sexual hang-ups."

"They're not hang-ups, Holger." It seemed to be Teresa's turn to be annoyed. "Those feelings are called desires. Every normal person has them."

Valissa walked away, suddenly not interested in the conversation of her friends. She had to admit, Teresa and Holger were the only people she associated with on a regular basis. In the beginning, she had chummed a little with the two sisters Naomi and Gabriella Lewis, but they were spending more and more time with Teresa's sons, Sigmund and Conrad. The four of them were Valissa's age, but she felt like a fifth wheel whenever she sat with the two couples, which happened less and less frequently.

As for the men who were ogling her, according to Teresa, she wasn't unaware of them. Did they really think just because Rob wasn't around she'd jump into bed with them?

She wasn't that desperate for sex, unlike Teresa, who talked about sex all the time. Most of the men were too old for her anyway, except Sigmund and Conrad, and they only had eyes for Naomi and Gabriella, which was how it should be.

She went back to her room and changed into her exercise outfit, a tight, formfitting bodysuit that left her legs and arms bare. Since she always felt somewhat naked wearing it because it revealed every detail of her slim figure, she threw a thin cape over her shoulders. When she entered the exercise room, there was only one other person in there. She recognized Wong. He was busy lifting weights. Valissa went to one of the treadmills and started running. Watching Wong, she had to admit it was obvious he lifted weights on a regular basis. His naked upper body rippled with muscles.

If she weren't engaged to Rob, she might even make a play for Wong. He was an attractive man.

She chided herself for even thinking it, but thoughts were not deeds. Besides, she had seen him in the company of that sex-goddess Cara Gunn. Nobody could compete with her. There were certain rumors going around about Cara and some of the men, and Valissa had no trouble believing there might be some truth to those rumors.

Wong seemed to be finished with his weightlifting. He came over to take the treadmill beside Valissa.

"Trying to stay in shape?" he asked, giving her a friendly smile.

She nodded without slowing her pace. "There's nothing else to do around here," she said, raising her voice to make herself heard over the droning of the treadmill. "I need to be physically active to stay healthy.

You know what they say: A healthy body is a healthy mind." She smiled. "I don't want to look into the mirror and close my eyes because I hate to see my out-of-shape lumpy body."

"The way you look there's no danger you'll have to close your eyes." He moved his eyebrows up and down and grinned, like a teenage boy trying to impress a girl he admires with a flattering statement but covering it up by making it sound funny.

Her face became hot the way it always did when a man gave her a compliment about the appearance of her body. The strict religious rules her parents imposed on her when she grew up still lingered in her subconscious mind, even though she tried hard to be more open and cast away the shackles the religion of her parents put on her. She could still hear her mother. "A woman should not display her body to a strange man. Only her husband should see her unclothed."

Unclothed also meant no tight bodysuits, like the one she wore right now while exercising. However, her parents and their religion were millions of kilometers away on another planet. They would never again dictate what she should wear or how she should behave. The feeling of freedom was great, but she also felt homesick. She missed the love she had shared with her family.

She looked up when she heard Wong talking. "Did I violate some kind of taboo with what I just said?"

She shook her head. "No, you didn't. It's been a while since a man complimented me on my looks. I mean other than my fiancé Rob. I remembered what my parents kept telling me, that's all."

"Where are your parents?"

"On Nu-Eden. They're farmers. I just realized I will never see them again. Ever."

"Perhaps you will. You can't lose hope."

"I have no such illusions. Even though the Xandra promised not to turn the second wave of settlers into her creatures, including some of the people from the first wave, the ones she left unchanged. My family was among the lucky ones; at least they were when I left Nu-Eden. But can you trust the Xandra? She's an alien entity and thinks on different levels than us humans."

"I only know about the Xandra from what I was told, so I can't comment. Is she really so powerful and has the ability to create clones from living people and transfer their minds into these clones? Can she actually influence people's minds?"

Wong slowed the speed of his treadmill and let it come to a halt. He stepped off the belt and moved in front of Valissa's machine. She reasoned he did that so he could look directly at her without craning his neck. It also gave him a better view of her body, making her self-conscious again.

"I experienced what she can do firsthand," she said, remembering her first sexual encounter with Rob. At the time, she thought it was nothing but a lucid dream, until she found out differently. Both, she and Rob, had been under the spell of the Xandra. She had done things she'd never do while conscious and awake and in control of what she said and did. As she thought about those things, she sensed her cheeks heating up again.

She wiped her hand across her forehead. "I'm getting hot from this vigorous exercise," she said breathlessly, trying to cover up her embarrassment.

"You don't have to exercise to look hot," Wong said, giving her his boyish grin again. His remark didn't help.

She laughed nervously. "Are you flirting with me, Mister Wong?"

"Mister Wong?" He tilted his head, his expression serious. "My name is Len. Don't call me Mister. It makes me feel old." He chuckled. "It isn't difficult to flirt with you. I'm sure all the unattached men, perhaps even some attached ones, have flirted with you. You're a beautiful girl."

She reduced the speed of her treadmill but kept walking at a slower rate. "I'm also engaged to a wonderful man whom I love with all my heart."

"I know, but Rob isn't here."

"That doesn't mean I'm forgetting about him. I'm certain he is not forgetting about me, either. Our love is probably the only thing helping him to endure what he's going through at this moment. Who knows what kind of awful things he has to face." She gave Wong a challenging look. "He's a very brave man and doing what most men on the Station were afraid to do."

"I'm not going to challenge your statement because you're right, Rob is a brave man. I question his motives for going, though. He didn't even know Regina. Why did he go into unknown danger to search for a woman who means nothing to him? Why did he leave you alone?"

Valissa stepped from the treadmill, silent for a moment. How could she answer Wong's question when she didn't know the answer herself? Why did Rob leave her alone with all these strangers?

"I guess he's concerned about other people's welfare. Back on Nu-Eden he went to search for my sister-in-law after she ran away into the jungle when nobody else cared to follow her. He's just that kind of a man."

"I would never have done that if you were my fiancée," Wong insisted in pursuing the subject. "Like I said, he doesn't even know Regina. Perhaps there were other reasons? Something you're not telling me? Was everything all right between you two?"

"Of course everything was all right. Still is." She felt like shouting at Wong for even suggesting she and Rob may have had problems. "You're right. There was another reason. He wanted to find out more about this Dark Goddess who is supposed to live somewhere underground."

Wong nodded solemnly. "I see. The Sras and the Jnaar talked about an evil entity living in the underground caverns. They called her worshippers Shadow-dwellers. Why would Rob be so interested in an alien goddess?"

"Because she sounds a lot like the Xandra on Nu-Eden. He's worried this Dark Goddess might be the equivalent of the Xandra."

"If she is, what's he going to do about her?" Wong shook his head. "I would think after escaping the influence of one alien entity he would stay far away from anything remotely similar."

"One would think so." Valissa had to agree. She shrugged and heaved a loud sigh. "But that's Rob. I tried to talk him out of it. He wouldn't listen. He told me something is compelling him to find out the truth about this Dark Goddess."

"He sounds like a man driven by something."

"He's not a fanatic, if that's what you mean," Valissa defended Rob.

Wong held up both hands. "I'm not saying that. I've never really spent much time with Rob, so I can't say I know him well. I'm sure he's a competent man and knows what he's doing. Let's hope he survives and comes back safely."

Valissa picked up her cape. "I'm going to hit the showers." Wong's eyes had followed her as she bent to get her cape and she could almost see the disappointment in his face when she covered her upper body with it. "I'll see you around."

"Wait." He reached out with the obvious intention of touching her arm, but changed his mind at the last moment. "Listen, Dr. Renaldo and I are taking the Landroamer this afternoon to investigate something in the forest. Jennifer Ratzenberger is also accompanying us. She's a biologist. Would you be interested in coming with us?"

"What are you going to investigate?"

"Some peculiar animals Dr. Renaldo apparently saw. I'm not quite sure."

"Why would you want me along? I know nothing about peculiar animals."

"Neither do I. My specialty is computers not animals." Wong shrugged. "I'm only going along as the driver."

"What would be my function?"

"Your function would be to look beautiful and grace us with your presence." Wong gave her a disarming smile.

She laughed when she saw his innocent expression. "You're making me suspicious. Too many compliments. Will we have to go outside? It's very cold out there."

"We have the best insulated cold weather suits money can buy. At least they were the best seven years ago when they were purchased. It'll be fun and a change from the daily boring routines. Look at you, exercising every morning, taking a shower, having lunch, spending a boring afternoon watching holograms, sometimes the same ones, or having boring conversations with boring people. Then going for supper, after that a boring evening, and then to bed alone. The same routine starts the next day. You should jump at the chance to do something different."

Valissa rolled her eyes. "The way you describe my life here sounds even more boring. I'm tempted, but—"

"What?"

"How would it look? I mean—you and I, we aren't really friends who hang out."

"No, we're not, but we could become good friends. In fact, we should, because my best friend, Hunter, is probably bonding with your fiancé. So it makes only sense that you and I also spend some time together."

"You make it sound so logical and simple. And tempting."

She had to admit, she was tempted. Life on the Station had become a boring routine, and a change would give her a chance to think of other things besides missing Rob.

She nodded, pursing her lips. "Okay. I'll come with you. As long as there're no strings attached."

"Fine. And don't worry. Nobody expects anything from you as payment, including me. We'll leave shortly after lunch. Meet us in the supply room so we can outfit you with a suit." He looked her up and down. "You are tall for a girl, you know."

"I know. I'm 165 centimeters."

"Like I said tall. I'm only three centimeters taller."

She chuckled softly. "You're actually short for a man."

Wong pulled a face. "After all the compliments I gave you? Do you have to rub it in?"

"But you're so muscular. It makes you look bigger." As her gaze wandered down his body, she felt her cheeks going red again when she noticed the large bulge in his small, tight briefs.

He was probably big down there, too, by the looks of it. She couldn't stop herself from thinking about it. A month without Rob and no sex gave rise to crazy thoughts.

"I'll be there," she said, turning and walking away quickly to cover her embarrassment.

"One o'clock," he called after her. "Be there at one o'clock."

As she stood in the shower, she had sudden doubts about going. What would Rob think if he knew what she was about to do? But then she chided herself. What was she actually doing? She was only going on a trip in the Landroamer with three other people. That's all. She wasn't cheating on Rob, and she wasn't doing anything wrong.

She made up her mind then and there. She'd go. Suddenly, she was looking forward to getting away from the Station for a few hours.

When she told Teresa at lunchtime about it, the older woman raised a delicate eyebrow and smiled enigmatically. "He's a handsome man, that Wong. Missing a few centimeters in height to make him a real hunk, but you could do worse."

"What do you mean by that?" Valissa demanded. "I have no interest in him."

"No? You accepted his invitation."

"He told me himself, there were no strings attached. He just wants to be my friend."

Teresa and Schreiber burst out laughing. "Honey, let me fill you in on what men really want." Teresa bent forward and lowered her voice a little. "Men are not interested in a platonic relationship with a woman, especially one as pretty as you. They may say they are, but all they really want is your pussy. If you're smart and horny enough, you'll let Wong have it. Your man won't be back for months and a healthy young woman like you needs to feel a man inside her once in a while. You need to work up a sweat underneath a man or…" She chuckled. "Or on top of him if you prefer. You'll need to let go of your inhibitions and let your juices flow, or you'll end up suffering from some kind of neurosis. Your body needs to balance those hormones for your mind to stay healthy."

Valissa stared at the older woman. "Are you suddenly some kind of psychiatrist?"

"Actually, I studied to be one before I married my late husband, but mostly I am talking about myself." She sighed and smiled sadly. "It's been quite some time since I had a man moan into my ears while he labors between my clenching thighs. I've always had a strong sex-drive. I admit I need a man badly." Her eyes flicked to Schreiber. "The only male friend I have on the Station is not interested in giving me what I want and need. You're lucky, honey, a man wants you and that thing between your legs that makes you a woman. My advice is give it to him. You can only benefit."

Valissa shook her head. "I won't cheat on Rob. I could never forgive myself."

"Give it a couple more months and you'll be climbing the walls. By that time, Wong may not be interested in you anymore. He may go back to that black-haired walking pussy Cara Gunn. I've seen them together, and it's obvious what she's giving him."

Schreiber gave a little chuckle. "She's giving him what she's giving every man who wants it."

"Then I have nothing to worry about. Wong gets his sexual satisfaction from Cara, and I'll give him my friendship." Valissa bestowed a triumphant smile on Teresa. "I can live with that."

"What about your sexual satisfaction?"

"That's why I exercise. It keeps my body in shape and my hormones balanced. It also keeps me from thinking the wrong thoughts."

"Do you moan during your exercise and scream when you're done?" Teresa asked.

"Of course not. Why would I?"

"You would if it made you feel good. I moan during the only exercise I prefer and scream at the end when my partner digs his hands into my buttocks and holds me against him until he's done."

"I never scream," Valissa said, blushing.

"Well, don't feel bad, not all women do. Some only whimper. Do you at least move and moan a little when you have sex with a man?"

Valissa clenched her fists as she thought of Rob and the pleasure she experienced when they made love.

Of course she moved. She was a passionate woman. She moaned when she had an orgasm, but now she couldn't even remember how it actually felt to have one. She felt so alone sometimes and missed Rob terribly. She missed the way he looked at her. She missed his strong arms holding her at night.

"Why are we talking about this?" she said in a low, almost subdued voice.

"Yes, why are we?" Schreiber chimed.

"Because it's natural to talk about the things we don't have and miss. I'm just trying to give some advice to a friend who seems to need it." Teresa focused on Schreiber. "You and I have become pretty good friends, wouldn't you agree?"

Schreiber nodded. "Yes, we have."

"Don't friends do nice things for each other? Don't friends usually try to make their friends feel good?"

"I suppose so. What are you getting at?"

"Let me put it bluntly. You're a man, on the outside anyway and have the equipment to make me feel good. What if I asked you to come to my room and sleep in my bed tonight? Just hold me for a while and use that male equipment of yours to make me happy. Would you do that for a friend? For me? You might even enjoy it."

Schreiber gave her a thoughtful look. "I would do that for you, but my male equipment may not work. Women don't excite me."

"By the tail of the comet! We don't even have to have the lights on. You could pretend I'm a man. My mouth and my buttocks wouldn't feel any different in the dark from those of a man. You just have to move a little lower with your pleasure maker before you insert it. Where there is a will there is a way."

"Perhaps there is no will."

"I remember you telling Rockwell at the orientation meeting you would consider contributing to the gene pool of our group. How did you think you could achieve that unless you had sex with a woman?" Teresa almost glared at Schreiber, obviously challenging him to give her a reasonable and satisfying answer. "I also remember you saying it wouldn't be a sacrifice. That means you would enjoy it."

"You're correct. I said that." Schreiber chuckled softly. "I only said it to annoy Rockwell."

"Are you saying you wouldn't enjoy having sex with me?"

Schreiber lifted his shoulders. "I don't know if I'd enjoy it or not. I've never been in that situation."

Teresa put her hand on his in an intimate gesture. "Maybe you should take me up on my invitation and find out. If nothing else, you'll spend a night with a friend in the same bed. What harm lies in that?"

"We may not be friend after that. I snore."

Teresa laughed. "So do I."

Valissa looked at the large clock on the wall. "I'd better go. I have fifteen minutes to get ready." She rose and looked around for Wong, hoping to find him at his usual table, but she didn't see him. He was probably already in the supply room getting things ready. She didn't want to be late.

Teresa's gaze remained serious. "Think about what I said, Valissa. Grab an opportunity when it comes and don't think too much about it. Follow your feelings and don't suppress your body's desires. If you do, someday they'll overwhelm you, and you'll do things you don't want to do but are forced to do. Life is like that."

"I'll give everything you said some thought." She walked away quickly, heading for her room.

When she got to the supply room, they were already waiting for her. Dr. Renaldo turned out to be a pleasant man, nearly as short as Wong, with a round face and hair hanging down to his shoulders, but the woman, Jennifer Ratzenberger, seemed a bit aloft at first impression. She was tall, towering over both men. Her body was thin, her face narrow, and her gray eyes as cold as steel, but when she smiled at Valissa, it lit up her face and eyes.

"So you're Wong's mystery date," Jennifer said.

"Is that what he called it? A date?" Valissa gave Wong a disapproving look.

Wong held up both hands. "In my defense, I never mentioned the word date."

"That's true, he never said date," Jennifer agreed. "I just assumed you were his new girlfriend."

Valissa shook her head. "I'm not that, either. I'm engaged to Rob Cameron."

"Isn't that the guy who went with Hunter to look for Regina?" Renaldo asked.

"That's him."

"I remember now seeing you with him," Jennifer said. She gave Valissa an apologetic smile. "Rumors are that you colonists are supposed to form only a loose relationship in order to keep the gene pool diversified—one woman has children with different men. So I just presumed. I meant no offense."

"That's okay. By the way, my name is Valissa."

"I'm Jennifer. Welcome to our little group. I assume Wong filled you in why we are going on this outing?"

"He did. Apparently, Dr. Renaldo spotted some peculiar animals."

"Not apparently." Renaldo chuckled good-humoredly. "I did see something when I scanned the area a few days ago. Unfortunately, the computer could not enhance the images sufficiently for me to make out details. What I think I saw was a flock of large, black birds. They burst from the trees and settled back into the thick branches moments later. Something spooked them, and it would be interesting to discover what kind of animal is roaming the forest in this cold weather, not to mention the birds, if they were birds."

"Here," Wong said, handing Valissa a bundle. "This suit should fit you. Try it on while I look for a pair of boots for you."

Valissa unfolded the bundle and noticed it was the same type of cold weather suit she had worn when they left the space shuttle that brought them to this planet. When she slipped into it, she discovered it fit her perfectly, unlike that other one. Wong brought a pair of insulated boots. They also felt comfortable when she put them on.

The others were already dressed in their outfits. They had, obviously, been waiting for her.

"I'm ready," she said, not wanting to be the one holding them back.

"Good. So are we." Renaldo looked at Wong. "How about all the stuff I requested?"

"Already stowed away safely on the Roamer."

"Well, let's go then." Renaldo grabbed a small backpack and threw it across his shoulder. "We don't have much time. I don't want to get caught in the dark coming back."

Valissa had never been inside the Landroamer and was surprised how roomy and comfortable it was inside. Wong drove it into the elevator. When the doors opened again, he eased it out of the tower onto the snow outside. The Landroamer slid silently across the snow surface as they headed for the distant forest.

She was still a little apprehensive about going on this trip, but when she looked out of the rear window at the giant egg floating above the white snow, she was happy to have accepted Wong's invitation. She had been cooped up far too long inside the research station that more and more seemed like a prison to her than a refuge from the harsh elements.

About the Author

Herbert Grosshans lives near Winnipeg, Canada. He spends much of his free time spinning tales about imaginary worlds and the strange creatures inhabiting them. His first published story "The Anniversary Gift" appeared in *Sweet Revenge* published by Midnight Showcase. Even though he writes in other genres, his love is Science Fiction. He enjoys building alien worlds and societies. Most of his stories contain an element of Erotica. To this date, he has published 27 books with Melange Books, not including this one. Please, visit Herbert's websites and blogs to find out more about him and his writing.

Websites: http://www.fictitioustales.weebly.com/
Blogs: http://www.hegro.blogspot.com/
http://www.hergros.blogspot.com/

Connect with Herbert on FaceBook, Pinterest, and Twitter.

FaceBook: http://facebook.com/hergros/
Pinterest: http://pinterest.com/herbertg/pins/
Twitter: http://www.twitter.com/hergros/

**Books by Herbert Grosshans available at Melange Books, LLC
www.melange-books.com**

Orola, Warrior Priestess
Bullet of Revenge
Dual Visions
Orion – Symbiont of Passion
Mark of the Cobra

Anthologies
Time Flares
Tapestry of Dreams

Series

Web of Conspiracy
Book One: Death of a Hero
Book Two: Traitors and Patriots
Book Three: Tarnished Valor

Stars in Chains
Book One: Slave
Book Two: Liberator

Seeds of Chaos
Book One: Eden's Gate
Book Two: Hell's Gate

Stardogs
Book One: Return to Redsky
Book Two: Redemption

The Spider Wars
Outpost Epsilon
Epsilon
Epsilon City
Raptor's Tooth
Codename Salamander

The Xandra
Book One: Daughter of the Dark
Book Two: Mother of Light
Book Three: Goddess of Life
Book Four: Lure of Seduction
Book Five: Escape from Paradise
Book Six: Iceworld

www.ingramcontent.com/pod-product-compliance
Lightning Source LLC
Chambersburg PA
CBHW020127180626
46810CB00004B/1428